FARRAGO

JAMES GARTON

Farrago
Copyright © 2024 by James Garton

Cover image: Elena Elisseeva / Alamy Stock Photo

All rights reserved. No part of this publication may be reproduced, distributed, or transmitted in any form or by any means, including photocopying, recording, or other electronic or mechanical methods, without the prior written permission of the author, except in the case of brief quotations embodied in critical reviews and certain other non-commercial uses permitted by copyright law.

Tellwell Talent
www.tellwell.ca

ISBN
978-1-998454-94-5 (Paperback)
978-1-998454-95-2 (eBook)

PART ONE

ACCIDENTS WILL HAPPEN

CHAPTER 1

SYLVIA

When she arrived at the underground car park beneath Sam Newbold's apartment building Sylvia carefully scraped the Corolla's front fender against a concrete pillar as she parked, hoping to mask the dents from the crash. She checked that there was no blood on the car, then sat for a moment taking several deep swallows from a flask of rum and Coke.

The damage to the car was more extensive than she had expected. Maybe Sam would know how to get the damage fixed on the quiet.

In the elevator to his apartment she checked her hair in the mirrors, and touched up her lipstick. Sam hugged her at the door, gave her a glass of wine, then stood with her at the picture window looking across the city lights in the driving rain.

"Everything OK?" he asked quietly when they sat down on the huge leather couch in front of the TV.

"Yes, except that I bashed into one of those concrete pillars in your car park."

"That's OK. I'll take care of it. How bad is the damage to your car?"

"Doesn't look too bad," Sylvia said hesitantly.

They settled down to watch Seinfeld on TV, a show that Sylvia loathed, but she said nothing as she thought about what to say next. After a few minutes she leaned over to Sam and said quietly, "To tell the truth, I dinged someone's car in the dark on the way over here. And I didn't stop to leave a note."

Sam turned to her and laughed.

"So much for smashing into the concrete pillar! OK, no problem. My driver knows a guy who will fix your car for cash, no questions asked. I'll take care of that for you," he said.

That was good to hear, and after a few drinks she went to bed with him, feeling relieved. The Corolla was her father's twenty-first birthday present to her, the first time Victor had ever been able to give her anything expensive, and she didn't want him to know that it was damaged.

She was lucky that Sam was a regular customer at Café Lorenzo, and that she'd had the opportunity to get to know him. She had no one else to turn to.

Sylvia knew from the time Sam rang the café to ask her out that a date with him could change her life. He was a handsome man, blonde hair and blue eyes, a rising star in the Labour Party. Only average height, though, but she didn't like heels anyway.

After dinner in an expensive restaurant, Sam's driver picked them up outside the minute they appeared, and she allowed herself to be swept along in comfort, all the way to Sam's penthouse, with its underground car park, luxurious fittings, and an amazing view of the city from his balcony.

They had a few drinks and she stayed the night. Sam Newbold was a lovely man, she decided, although somewhat scrawny. He was pigeon-chested, too, with little body hair and the sort of limp white flesh that needed an expensive suit to disguise his lack of bone and muscle.

However, Sam was charming and funny, making her feel like someone special, rather than the underpaid waitress she actually was. And he was very generous, just the person to help her out with the situation her sister Naomi was in.

The last time Sylvia heard from Naomi she had left home and was supposed to be sharing an apartment with a girlfriend in Geelong. But instead she had been shacked up with Charlie Triado, ignoring Sylvia's warning to stay away from him.

"You're just jealous because Charlie dumped you and then asked me out," Naomi had said. "You don't even live at home any more. What do you care?"

"No, I'm not jealous," Sylvia had replied. "It's because Charlie's a total ratbag, and he's too old for you."

Some things never changed, and Naomi was one of them.

This time around, the predictable had happened. "Charlie just disappeared," Naomi sobbed into the phone. "When I woke up one morning he was gone."

"When was this?"

"About two weeks ago."

"Did he give you any warning?"

"No, no-oh," she wailed. "He just left a note." And she sobbed some more, heaving gasps of breath and blowing her nose into a tissue.

"And what did the note say?" asked Sylvia patiently.

"That he had paid the rent till the end of the month, and I could stay in the apartment until then."

"No forwarding address, no phone number?"

"No."

"Do you know where he works?"

"I rang his work number, but they said he resigned a month ago." Naomi was crying uncontrollably again, and obviously couldn't cope with any more questions. It was a well-planned escape. Charlie could have gone anywhere, maybe to Sydney, where he had some friends.

Sylvia went to Geelong and helped Naomi to move back home, Naomi a crying mess in her bathrobe, left in the near empty apartment waiting to be evicted. Sylvia rang their father, and told Victor what had happened, then took her home to Melbourne to face the inevitable protracted bitter silence from her mother.

At that point Sylvia decided to wait and see when Charlie would turn up next. It was a safe bet he would return to Melbourne at some time when he felt the coast was clear, and sure enough Naomi rang with the news from a friend who had seen him.

"Charlie's back in Melbourne, working in his father's real estate office again," Naomi said with a quiver in her voice. "What'll I do?" She sounded numb and detached, which at least was an improvement on hysteria.

"I'll talk to him," Sylvia said, with no clear idea of how she would go about it. Someone had to confront him, though, and after a while she came up with a plan.

It was better to catch up with Charlie as soon as possible before he moved again. Sylvia rang Triado Real Estate and said she was returning a call to Charlie, and the receptionist put her straight through.

"Hello, Charlie. It's been a long time."

"Is that you, Sylvia?"

"It certainly is," she said, calm and friendly.

"Good to hear from you," Charlie said. Typical of him to brazen it out. "To what do I owe the pleasure?" he added in a joking tone.

Sylvia felt like spitting, but carried on calmly. "Well, now that you've split with Naomi, I thought that we should catch up again. Let bygones be bygones, like they say."

"Oh, right. Good to hear it. How about a drink tonight?" He was still cautious, but Sylvia could hear the anticipation in his voice.

"Well, I was thinking more of a quiet chat. Perhaps tomorrow night. Somewhere comfortable."

"Yeah, OK. Where would you like to go?"

"How about our favourite motel? Like the good old days?"

"Really? Are you sure?" Charlie sounded uncertain, so Sylvia laughed quietly to reassure him.

"Absolutely. I've missed you, Charlie. Be good to catch up again. Tomorrow night OK? Seven o'clock?"

"Yeah, sure, sounds good." He sounded relieved, and the anticipation was back in his voice.

"Terrific. Maybe you could make a booking for us? Then park your car outside the room so I can find you. What are you driving?"

"A white Ford Falcon."

"No worries. Don't be late!"

"I'll be there on the dot," Charlie said, and Sylvia could hear him grin. Apparently she wasn't too old for him just yet. What he needed was a taste of his own medicine.

Sylvia decided not to give Sam any details about her plan for dealing with Charlie Triado, but rather she would act first, then enlist his help later.

***

Rain was spattering the windscreen, driven by a cold southerly breeze. Very little traffic, and no pedestrians. A perfect night for what she had in mind.

She parked across the road from the motel and waited for Charlie's car to show up, pulling on the baseball cap she had bought that morning, her long hair tucked up inside it, and sank down in her seat to avoid being seen.

A few minutes later, Charlie's white Ford cruised past, its engine a low rumble, and parked in the car park near the flickering red neon sign that said "Motel". Sylvia pushed the gear stick into Drive and followed him in at a distance, driving slowly with her wipers running and her lights off. With hands tight on the steering wheel, she accelerated as Charlie got out of his car, door open. Flicking her headlights on full beam, she swung her car towards him. Dazzled, Charlie put one hand up to shade his eyes from the glare.

Sylvia sideswiped his car with her front fender, metal scraping against metal, slamming into Charlie and hurling him to the ground. She hit the brakes and skidded on the wet bitumen, nearly colliding with a parked SUV.

Glancing at the side mirror Sylvia could see Charlie lying in a heap, still and silent. Was he dead, or not? She slammed the car into reverse, hung her head out the car window, and reversed with a screech of tyres at Charlie's prone figure. The Corolla went over him like a speed bump, throwing her up in her seat, her seat belt tightening, then down again as she skidded to a stop and peered through the windscreen at his body, the wipers twitching back and forth.

Charlie was lying spreadeagled on the bitumen in a puddle, his face turned towards her, eyes wide-open, expressionless, his legs at an angle, rain pouring down on him.

He looked dead now, but she couldn't hang around to make sure.

"That'll teach you, you bastard," she muttered.

She did a U-turn, switched off her lights and accelerated as the reception clerk ran out of the office, stopping at the roadside to watch her as she drove off down the street.

At the next intersection she switched her lights on again and joined the traffic in Beach Road. The car was running smoothly, the impact of hitting Charlie appeared to have had no effect. She took off the baseball cap and threw it out the window, then switched on the CD player and lit a cigarette with the car lighter.

The rain was a perfect cover for her. The motel clerk had no hope of seeing her number plate clearly, and her navy blue Corolla was probably one of the hundreds trawling about Melbourne at that very moment. At most he would have seen a driver of indeterminate age and sex wearing a baseball cap. Any report he gave to the police wouldn't give them much to go on.

CHAPTER 2

HARRY

When I finally catch up with her, I find Melissa Frankel living in an Edwardian villa off fashionable Kooyong Road in Toorak, silvertail territory. A gravel driveway leads to an ornate steel security door shielding heritage glass from intruders.

She answers the doorbell promptly, wearing the same uniform of jeans and pullover I remember from student days. I was a first year student back then in 1972, and she was in the final year of her law degree, a few years older than me. That means that she must be in her late forties by now.

She doesn't look it. A little silver in her curly black hair, the same freckles around her nose, and that quizzical expression, the direct gaze as fiercely intelligent and energetic as ever. Every inch the smart human rights lawyer I've seen on TV.

"Harry Mott," I say.

"Ah, Harry. Come in. Sorry I didn't recognize your name when we spoke on the phone. It's been a long time."

"Yes, nearly twenty five years."

She must have asked around about who the hell I am. I doubt that I made any impression on her all those years ago, a skinny kid with long hair and a thin beard, lost in the crowd of student protestors she hung out with.

Melissa smiles warmly, and leads me to a comfortable sitting room lined with bookshelves. She waves me to a chair, and we sit facing each other across a glass-topped coffee table.

"So you said on the phone you wanted to talk about Sam Newbold?" she says, eyebrows raised.

"I work for some of Sam's colleagues. They have concerns about Sam's political activities when he was a student."

"Really? What activities in particular?"

"The anti-Vietnam War demonstrations. Back in the day when you both were Maoists, and in a relationship." No point dithering around.

Melissa laughs. "What are they worried about? That was a long time ago."

"The past can be tricky, especially for successful politicians. There's a lot hanging on it. There's talk of Sam being appointed as Leader of the Opposition, especially after his recent TV interview."

"Yes, that was an interesting load of bullshit," she says. She doesn't ask me what my role is. I guess it's obvious.

I look out at the luxuriant garden which cleverly explores the boundary between landscape gardening and benign neglect. Three small silver birch trees huddle together over a bird bath, their bare branches glistening in the cold winter rain.

Everything about the house and garden speaks for the studied ease of someone accustomed to the best of everything, but choosing to live simply.

"Sam spoke in the interview like we were just draft resisters back then, almost as though what we did was a student prank," Melissa says. "When in fact we were members of the Maoist Party, Communists, totally opposed to US imperialism, and we believed in the Revolution. We supported the North Vietnamese communist regime, and sent them donations."

I nod, and wait. She hasn't offered me a cup of coffee, so I assume I'll be leaving soon.

A Yorkshire terrier appears beside her armchair, and she scoops it up and sits it on her lap. It watches me anxiously, trying to calculate what sort of threat I am.

I don't say anything, remembering the dictum that the art of listening requires at least a skerrick of silence. I'm wondering if she has a partner, but there's no sign of anyone else around the house, nor any kids. Only the dog. God knows why she has such a useless little tyke. What she needs in a house this affluent is something more substantial, like Peter, the hefty black mongrel of my childhood, guarding our rickety front fence with loud barks and impressive teeth.

"Sam was a great speaker," she continues. "And still is. Back then at demos you could stick him in front of a crowd of five or ten thousand, wind him up, and he'd be off and running. But the sight of cops turned him to water. He was a complete fucking coward when it came to physical confrontation."

I nod, and wait some more.

"Pretty much everything in Sam's TV interview is invention," Melissa said. "Sam didn't go into hiding in a shack up in the High Country, like he claims. In fact I drove Sam down the Great Ocean Road in my mother's car to our beach house, and he lived there like a king for several months, a glorified holiday."

She lights a cigarette, and then resumes her story.

"I'd drive down on weekends to visit Sam with food and clean clothes. He couldn't even look after himself, like going shopping or doing laundry. He spent most of his time reading crime novels and ringing up his mates to invite them to stay for a few days."

There's no reason to doubt what she says. I light a cigarette myself, and Melissa pushes an ashtray towards me.

"Sam was bored out of his mind down at the beach," she continues. "Any time I went there he was constantly checking out the windows for unmarked Special Branch cars, nervous as hell. In fact he was a wreck, not sleeping, jittery. A bit different to the romantic twaddle in his interview."

It seems strange to me to be sitting there listening to this fierce, energetic woman, still bristling with revolutionary ardour after decades of activism, confronting the police on the streets, getting bashed, and hauled into court, then becoming a successful lawyer and beating them all at their own game. The fact that she once believed in some sort of apocalyptic revolution doesn't seem to worry her now, nor that she still actively supports communist dictators. After all, she has never disavowed Maoism. What can possibly be driving her, daughter of a wealthy surgeon, a graduate of the best schools and universities?

"Why would Sam lie about his activities? When it's so easy to disprove?" I ask her.

"Well, it's not actually that easy," she says. "His word against ours. I suspect that Sam believes that what he's said is true. He's replayed it all in his head a thousand times, and he's come to believe his version of events."

"What do you think will be the response amongst your colleagues to all this?"

"Sam was written off as a turncoat a long time ago. He's a member of the Labour party now, for Christ's sake! He wants to be Leader of the Opposition, after all. And who knows what else in the future? Premier of Victoria? Prime Minister? Not our problem. More a problem for the Labour Party."

She's silent for a moment, as if deciding whether or not to say something more.

"There's one thing I will say to you, Harry," she finally says. "But you'll have to keep your source secret."

"OK," I say, my ears pricking up. "What is it?"

"There were rumours that we had a police spy in our group, the inner circle of our Maoist faction. Special Branch detectives had been arriving at our meeting places before we got there. We noticed the buggers actually waiting for us. So we laid a trap, giving different times to our comrades, and guess who the informer turned out to be?"

"Not Sam Newbold?"

"Yes, that's right. It was hard to take, but we decided to ride with it, feed him bullshit, and use him for disinformation. For me it wasn't an easy thing to do with someone I was in a relationship with. I'd been living with Sam for about a year around that time. It was a roller coaster ride with him, anyway, but discovering that he was a police spy was the last straw."

I nod, watching her, wondering how much she was driven by personal animosity. Whatever the reason, Melissa and her mob of Maoists from back in the day are now well and truly ditching Sam Newbold, despite the secrets they have kept for so many years.

"You'll pass this on to the Party bosses?" she asked.

"Yes. But we need to keep it under wraps, until a decision is made," I say, watching her face closely.

"So they're going to blackmail him, rather than expose him?"

"Yes," I say. No point in lying. Melissa knows how these things work.

She pushes the dog gently off her lap, and I put out my cigarette in the ashtray. She sees me to the front door, apologizing again for not recognizing me from all those years ago when we were students. And she says goodbye and let me know how it goes, without really meaning it.

"If you have any more questions, you can contact me at my office," she adds as I turn to go. Very business-like. So no offer of the number for her mobile phone or her home landline. It's the briefest of visits to a distant past, much of it long forgotten.

***

When Rita asks me about my day that evening at dinner, I simply tell her that I've been checking the background of a prominent Labour politician. "I knew him at uni," I say. Which is simplifying things, but near enough.

"Oh, when you were rioting in the streets on those anti-war demos," she says with a laugh.

"Something like that."

Our son Jesse is out somewhere, probably playing guitar with his garage band mates. For a moment I wish he is home, the polite, quizzical teenager, joining in our dinner time talk, the dead spit of Rita. Sometimes I feel like he is the adult, and I am the teenager. However, a quiet pleasant dinner alone with Rita is always a bonus. Whether I acknowledge it or not, problems usually come into perspective when we talk.

"And? What's going to happen to this politician?" Rita asks.

"He could be in a bit of strife."

"Aren't we all," Rita says. "The past has a way of catching up with you, don't forget that."

"Speak for yourself."

"Maybe he'll confess everything if you talk to him long enough. The whole truth and nothing but the truth."

"I doubt it," I say.

No seasoned politician ever talks about the trouble they got into in their youth, unless it's a lie to save their arse. And the student demonstrations against the Vietnam War are now ancient history and mostly forgotten, except for those who were there at the time. This leaves plenty of wriggle room to embroider the past.

CHAPTER 3

SYLVIA

"Where to?" Charlie asked Sylvia as they roared along in the fast lane in his hotted-up Commodore. He was driving casually with one hand, a muscular brown arm half out the open window.

"Not far from Moorabbin railway station."

"No worries," Charlie said with that brilliant smile.

It was a hot humid evening, with intermittent patches of rain, the car's tyres hissing on the wet surface of the road. A Saturday night, the Nepean Highway crowded with cars speeding home, drivers drunk as skunks from a day spent in the pub or boozing at backyard barbecues in the sunshine with burned sausages and endless cans of beer.

A car packed with several hoons tore past, headlights flashing, horn blaring, windows wound down so that loud rock music thumped out at them, drunken contorted faces shouting a challenge for a race.

Charlie ignored them, shaking his head, murmuring "Dickheads" as their car sped off, the passengers still yahooing out the windows, and their tail lights disappeared down the road.

Soon they swung off the highway with a squeal of tyres and she gave him more directions.

"Stop here," Sylvia said half a block from the shop.

"OK. See you next Saturday?"

"Yes," she said, kissing Charlie's cheek and sliding out the car door as he reached across to embrace her. It was too hot in the car, and anyway, she had only just met him that evening. Let him wait.

Sylvia found her mother, Naomi and Jack in front of the TV in their cramped lounge room, while her father was locked away in their dingy little shop doing the books.

"Did you have a nice time, dear?" Eileen asked, looking askance at her with her pale, cold eyes, but turning back to the TV before Sylvia answered that yes, she did have a nice time, poking her tongue out at Naomi who was grinning at her provocatively. Sitting at his mother's feet, absorbed in a comic, Jack didn't even look up, the spoiled little brat. She couldn't wait till next Saturday to go out with Charlie again, away from the silent disapproval of her mother.

Things would be different once she was living away from home. Anything would be possible. She could conduct her romance with Charlie out in the open, instead of sneaking around in secret. Eileen would have a major meltdown if she found out that Charlie was nearly ten years older than her. Her mother had a strict moral code, no exceptions.

When school finished at the end of the year, Sylvia spent the summer holidays with Charlie on the beach and in motel rooms along the bay. As the holidays ended, Charlie announced that he was going back to Vivian, his former girlfriend.

He wished Sylvia well, he said, when they were about to leave their room at their favourite motel near the beach at Mordialloc. He ducked the ashtray that Sylvia threw at his head, and ran for his car, leaving her screaming "You bastard! You bastard!" from the doorway.

She stood crying outside their room until the woman on the motel reception desk came and pushed her gently back inside and said that she had to get dressed and leave, immediately.

The humiliation of that moment still made her shake with rage, years later.

***

In the morning after the crash Sylvia woke up to find Sam's arm draped across her. He was lying with his head thrown back on the pillow, snoring lightly. She disentangled herself, waking him up, and kissed him on the cheek and offered to get coffee.

When she returned to the bedroom she gave Sam yet another amended version of the accident. "There's something else I didn't tell you," Sylvia said. "Actually, I knew the driver in the car I hit."

"How do you mean?"

"He's a guy who asked my kid sister out when she was still in school. Under age. And he raped her. I went to confront him, but he was going to drive off. Then I lost it and drove my car at him."

"Christ, what a bastard. Was he injured?"

"I think so, but I didn't get a good look. His name is Charlie Triado."

"OK, I think I can help you with that. The police will be involved, and I have contacts in the police union."

"You're not concerned? How it might bounce back on you, I mean?"

"No. Half the guys that work for me spend their time fixing this kind of thing."

"Oh, good. Thanks. I thought the Labour Party was full of the good guys?"

"Not likely. But no worse than the Coalition. Nothing but trouble some weeks, and occasionally it's big stuff. Fraudulent deals of one kind and another. Members associating with criminals. Theft of funds donated to the party. The list goes on."

"Sounds like fun."

"You should join the Party. You'd enjoy it."

"Politics is all boring meetings, isn't it?"

"Some of the time. But there's plenty of challenges, too."

"Not for me. I'm thinking of a career in real estate at the moment."

"Good for you," Sam said. "Let me know if I can help you with that. Anyhow, I'd better make a phone call."

He picked up one of those new mobile phones, an elegant little device that folded in half, and spoke into it for a moment or two.

"OK, all fixed," Sam said. "When my guy comes to pick up your car, he'll leave his car for you to use."

"Thanks, Sam."

"My pleasure."

Sam left soon after for work in a very smart suit and carrying a hefty briefcase, telling Sylvia to stay in his apartment all day if she wanted.

She rang Café Lorenzo on the landline to say she'd be off work for the day with a bad cold, and watched the TV over breakfast for any news about Charlie, catching a brief mention of a bayside hit-and-run and the accident victim being taken to hospital, then went back to bed.

In the afternoon she showered and dressed and drove home in the rain in the borrowed car. After dinner she locked herself in her room with a cask of cheap wine and played her BeeGees CD at full volume.

She ignored her housemates banging on the door to complain about the noise, then fell asleep and woke up hours later in the middle of the night, freezing cold and with a stiff neck.

***

The next day Sam rang her at the café and told her that everything had been taken care of.

"Your friend is still in hospital. His injuries sound quite serious. In fact, he still hasn't regained consciousness. However, I followed up with the contact I told you about, and everything is under control. The police are investigating your friend's dealings with under-age girls. He'll be lucky to squeeze out of this situation without being charged."

"Dealings with under-age girls?"

"That's what they call it. They'll be putting a lot of pressure on him."

"Thanks, Sam," Sylvia said quietly. She should have driven at Charlie faster.

Naomi rang her at home late that evening. Sylvia picked up the shared phone in the hallway, and heard a loud snuffling noise at the other end.

"He's dead, Sylvia, Charlie's dead!" Naomi was sobbing and gasping into the phone.

Sylvia waited a moment until she stopped, then said, "What happened?"

"A car accident. Hit-and-run. It was on the TV news. Didn't you know?"

"No, I didn't. We don't have TV here."

"You don't sound sad," Naomi said with a sob.

"Accidents will happen, Naomi. And Charlie wasn't a nice person. I don't feel sorry for him."

"Oh," Naomi said, and went on sobbing.

"Don't cry. He's not worth it."

Typical Naomi. God knows why she got into such a mess. If she had done as she was told and stayed away from Charlie, Sylvia wouldn't have sought him out again.

One thing was clear, though, it would have been impossible to square things off with Charlie without Sam Newbold's help.

At the same time, Sylvia had no illusions about relying on Sam. While she knew that their affair was the beginning of big changes for her, realistically she had to accept the limitations of a relationship that was conducted in the gaps between everything else in Sam's life.

It was obvious that his apartment was a bachelor pad, and that he didn't live there in any real sense. She knew that his life outside work was divided between a failing third marriage with a couple of kids and a mistress or two, and that she would be lucky if she could count herself as one of the latter.

As for the future, it was obvious that her relationship with Sam wouldn't last, and that she had to bank every advantage she could before time ran out.

CHAPTER 4

HARRY

When I arrive at Melbourne University in early 1972 I spend most of my time wandering lost around campus, marvelling at the lush green manicured lawns, the stately heritage buildings, the air thick with privilege, feeling like a foreigner in my own country.

The university is just a few kilometres from where I was born in the industrial suburbs on the wrong side of the Yarra River, and the campus is buzzing with private school freshers arriving for Orientation Week, plus a few ragtag scholarship students like myself. Little did I know that an exotic tribe of rich kids has been parked on my doorstep from before the time I was born.

On the last day of my second week on campus I'm having coffee and a cigarette in the Student Cafeteria with Anton Nakamura and a friend of his called Rita Kapernaros, two students I've met in my economics lectures. Rita is loud and happy, an extrovert with long black hair and a cackling laugh. She's an amusing contrast to Anton's restraint, an odd couple of mates.

It's near dusk, a hot and humid day now just simmering to a close, and we can see students gathered around a speakers' dais at one end of the Student Cafeteria building.

"Looks like some sort of demo," says Rita. "C'mon guys, let's take a look," so we go and see what's happening.

An intense looking woman with a pale freckled face, wearing a white tee shirt and jeans, is speaking into the microphone, her voice bouncing off the walls of the buildings surrounding us.

"Our next speaker is Sam Newbold, from Revolutionary Student Action," she says. "Sam is well known to many of you for his opposition to the Vietnam War. For several years now he has resisted the conscription that is sending young people to fight in Vietnam to support American imperialism. Victory for Vietnam is near, and we must do all we can to support the Viet Cong."

This is Melissa Frankel, I later find out, a leading student activist, an emphatic energetic figure up on the ramshackle wooden stage. Then Sam Newbold, long blonde hair and beard, green Army Disposals shirt with the sleeves rolled up, shorts and sandals, steps up onto the wooden rostrum, grabs the mic from Melissa and with a big grin shouts: "Thank you, thank you!" to get attention.

Then this Sam Newbold guy yells: "Are we all against conscription for the Vietnam War?"

"Yes we are!" comes from several voices scattered around the crowd. Probably mates of his.

"Let's hear it again. Are we all against conscription?"

"Yes we are!"

This time the crowd roars back in full voice, a couple of hundred university students, male and female, long hair, beards for the men, jeans and tee shirts. More students are joining the crowd to find out what's going on.

Sam raises his voice and punches the air. "Australian troops - including conscripts - are sent to Vietnam to support the American troops and their war crimes! Remember the My Lai massacre, when hundreds of innocent Vietnamese civilians were slaughtered by the US army!"

"This guy's good," Anton says beside me.

Sam is off again. "We must stop the Vietnam War, and we must support the Viet Cong and Ho Chi Minh!" he shouts.

"The Australian government..." Sam waits to allow the yelling to die down. "And this Australian government jails hundreds of draft resisters. People like the legendary John Zarb, sentenced to two years in Pentridge Prison, just down the road from where we are standing here. Anyone who refuses to be conscripted into so-called National Service for two years is sent to prison!" Groans and boos, many of them from males of conscription age.

It hits me then that my conscription call-up papers might well arrive after my twentieth birthday in about eighteen months' time, if my birth date is drawn out of the lottery barrel. Something I've barely thought about, it seems a long way off. All the same, I do know, very definitely, that I do not want to go into the Army and get sent to Vietnam.

Looking around the crowded quadrangle, students jammed up against the Cafeteria wall and leaning against the trees outside the sports centre, Sam yells again "Stop the war now!" then holds up the mic for them to shout.

"Stop the war now!" the crowd yells, as Sam waves his arms upwards like someone conducting an orchestra.

"Stop the war now! Stop the war now!" the crowd chants.

They keep it up, Sam waving the microphone at them and stepping down from the rostrum. Someone throws a beer bottle at the wall of the Cafeteria Building, and several more follow. Others start throwing the tables and chairs outside the Cafeteria against the wall, where they crash haphazardly into a mess of chair and table legs.

"That Sam Newbold guy is really something. And the girl too. What's their group called?" I ask Anton.

"Didn't she say Revolutionary Student Action?" he says.

"How about we join up?"

Rita says, "Not my scene. I'm not into breaking furniture," and she laughs. She looks attractive in a sort of peasant blouse and denim skirt, and I wish I could think of something to say to her.

"Aren't they Maoists or something?" Anton says.

"So what?" I say.

Anton shrugs, and it dawns on me that I know nothing about his politics. All I know about Anton is that he's gay and lives with his Mum in Maribyrnong, only an unfashionable suburb or so away from where I grew up.

However, I do know, instantly, that whoever these student activists are, I want to join them.

"I'm off home," Rita says. And she strides off in the direction of the Parkville side of campus. I watch her leave, feeling disappointed to see her go.

Within a couple of days Anton and I find a member of Revolutionary Student Action in a near derelict terrace house off Faraday Street. He's your classic radical intellectual, black framed glasses, long hair and beard, crushed jeans and Army Disposal jacket, with Bob Dylan screeching a protest song in the background. He's noncommittal and obviously not very interested in a pair of green freshers who don't know their Viet Cong from their Ho Chi Minh.

He shoves a couple of leaflets at us, takes a note of our names, swears us to secrecy, and Anton and I are now members of the most radical group of anti-war protestors on campus, or possibly in all Australia. I have no idea what I am getting into.

***

Going home on the tram at the end of the day after lectures becomes a disconcerting journey into my immediate past. Suddenly our tattered old street beside the railway line is painted a darker shade of grey. Even worse, our battered weatherboard house with my rickety sleepout out the back is like some tragic scene from the documentary on the Great Depression that we've been shown in economics tutorials. Inside the house is just as bad; torn lino, the scratched laminex kitchen table, outside toilet, a fridge as old as I am.

God knows what my parents make of me going off to university. Although I know that Sid and Billie are proud of me, it's obviously all a mystery to them.

I explain to Sid how I'm studying Keynesian economic theory, and who Lord Keynes was, but Sid looks dubious.

"That sort of stuff won't buy the baby a pram," he says.

"Stop your chuntering," Billie says to him, laughing and handing him a cup of tea.

"You'll need to get a job when all this larking about is over," Sid adds. He has a point. He left school at fourteen, and doesn't know a university from a hole in the ground, but then neither do I, and he's right. Where will it all end up? Either way, it's time to leave home.

And I figure out that I can afford to live in a share house near campus, if I supplement my scholarship with part-time work. So I get a job at the Cadbury warehouse in Collingwood packing display boxes for a couple of days a week. It's easy work, and my beer money has to come from somewhere. I live in a bare room with a mattress on the floor in a Carlton share house. It's one of the hundreds of tumbledown terrace houses owned by the Italian immigrants who arrived after the Second World War, now landlords in their own right since they began moving to greener pastures in the outer suburbs. My share house is within walking distance of campus, and the dozens of Italian cafés in Lygon Street.

On campus I'm surrounded by rich kids who arrive at university apparently fully formed. They are engaged in the next inevitable step towards life as a barrister, public intellectual, doctor, politician, CEO and so on, a progression as natural as a butterfly emerging from its chrysalis.

As for me, I am totally without ambition, and have no idea what I am going to do when the party's over.

***

Over the next few weeks after I sign on for Revolutionary Student Action all I get involved with is poster blitzes, sneaking around in the dark pasting anti-war posters onto telegraph poles, on the lookout for cops who never come.

But then Anton and I join our new revolutionary comrades in a demonstration against Bluestone Corporation, a multinational involved in manufacturing Agent Orange, stirring up some action at what started out as a peaceful protest. We aren't arrested, but we throw stones at the Bluestone headquarters building, and there's rumours about the police following up on the damage we cause.

Melissa Frankel calls a meeting that night at a share house in Carlton to review the demo.

When I arrive, Sam Newbold is standing by an old fan with a sheet of paper in his hand, talking to Melissa. It's an intense discussion, but I can't hear what they're saying. They are very secretive, and in any case, they pay little attention to people who don't belong to their inner circle.

The room is hot and the solitary small fan isn't making much difference. Anton joins me, and we sit together on uncomfortable rickety chairs at the back of the room.

More members file in, greeting each other and discussing the demo, all males, all with long hair and beards. By this time my own hair and beard have grown long enough for me to at least look like a member of the group.

Cans of beer are passed around, and an occasional joint. I take a beer, and pass up on the dope. I've tried it a couple of times at parties, and all it does is make me cough and feel drowsy.

Sam likes a joint, I notice, smoking pretty much every time I've seen him.

Melissa posts Anton out the front to watch the street for police surveillance, and calls on everyone to sit down. The group of a dozen or so students stop milling about and chatting, sitting quietly on the semicircle of chairs assembled facing the back wall.

Anton and I seem to be the only ones assigned sentry duties at these meetings. We're the newbies, amongst all these veteran activists, and we don't fit in anyway, so we get the shit jobs.

Melissa then opens the meeting, saying that the Bluestone demo is a success. Provoking police violence is a very successful tactic, she tells us, and getting arrested is a statement that can't be ignored, but unfortunately this time the cops were cautious, with no arrests, probably avoiding publicity on orders from Bluestone.

"We must show American corporations like Bluestone that we'll never give up the fight against US imperialism," Melissa says. "We must follow Mao in our resistance to American hegemony."

Then she goes on about President Nixon the war criminal, Watergate, US imperialism, the CIA, blah, blah, blah, and I drift off a little.

Then Melissa reaches her conclusion, eyes shining, her finger stabbing the air, and I sit up again.

"We proved again today that we provide the revolutionary activity, the broken windows that make news whenever anti-war demonstrations grow violent enough to interest the press. We have made our point about Bluestone's criminal involvement in producing Agent Orange, and we will keep on making our point until our troops are withdrawn from Vietnam."

I love Melissa's line about providing broken windows for the revolution. Taking a stand, showing them that we mean business.

I miss what Melissa says after that when Anton comes back inside and taps me on the shoulder. My turn as sentry.

The first thing I see when I step out the front door and look up and down the street is two men in suits sitting in a grey

Holden across the road under a street light, ties loosened in the heat. Obviously it's Special Branch detectives in an unmarked car, looking for all the world as though they want to be seen. Anton must be blind not to notice them.

When I come back in and interrupt Melissa to announce that we are under surveillance, it is probably the only time we will make eye contact for anything more than a few seconds in my whole glorious history as a Maoist revolutionary, all three months of it.

Melissa nods and calmly leads us as we all file out the back door, crawl through a gap in the side fence, cross someone's backyard, then sneak out into a side street at intervals.

I walk with Anton to catch his tram, chatting about the Special Branch detectives sitting in their car in the heat. Anton's tram clangs its bell in the distance, and we make it to the tram stop just in time.

"See you tomorrow in Cafe Lorenzo, three o'clock. Rita is coming too," he says, and leaps aboard the tram and waves out the window at me as it clatters away down Lygon Street, shattering the quiet night air like some nightmare monster, electricity pole swaying from side to side against the cable overhead, its lighted interior disappearing towards the Housing Commission flats.

I quickly walk the short distance to my share house across the road from the cemetery, nervously looking over my shoulder for any cops.

Large elaborate crosses stand above the gravestones, eerie in the moonlight, and it's a relief to get home and lock the door.

***

When I arrive at Café Lorenzo the next day, Anton is sitting at our usual table with his head in one of the local tabloids. He glances at me briefly and then holds up the paper for me to read the headline before I've even sat down: "Violent Demonstration by Student Thugs," it says. Then he starts reading the article to me:

A young lawyer at Bluestone Corporation, Mona Lippi, suffered a severe cut to her eyebrow from stones thrown at the windows of the corporation's building in the CBD this afternoon. University students demonstrating against the Vietnam War stormed the front doors of the building at around two pm, before police moved them on. A police spokesman said that most of the demonstrators were peaceful, but that the stones were thrown by a small violent minority, who could not be identified in the melee. Miss Lippi was taken by ambulance to Royal Melbourne Hospital, where she is under sedation. Hospital authorities say that there are concerns for the sight in her left eye.

"Look!" Anton says when he finished reading, and turns the newspaper around to face me.

I bend forward and look at the photo. There's Mona Lippi, short brown hair and a thin face, with a determined look despite the bandage wrapped around her head. And then Anton puts the newspaper down on the table and raises an eyebrow at me.

"Hello to you too," I say.

"We did that," says Anton, pointing at the photo.

"No, we didn't! I threw stones at those second storey windows. And so did Sam Newbold and Melissa Frankel, and several others. But you didn't."

"Nevertheless…" Anton says.

"It's all cooked up. Don't worry about it."

He's frowning, and staring into his coffee. Around us people are chatting, and a group of students arrives at the table next to us, scraping their chairs noisily and laughing loudly at some joke as they sit down. Anton and I are sitting there in glum silence, the only two people in Café Lorenzo who aren't enjoying themselves.

The newspaper report is typical right-wing tabloid press sensationalism, but it doesn't help the Cause for half of Melbourne to read about a young lawyer "blinded" by our assault on the

Bluestone Corporation building. And very likely it would be kept in the public eye for as long as possible by the capitalist press.

"What'll we do?" Anton says slowly.

"The cops haven't got anything on us, or they would have laid charges," I say. "In all the confusion at the demo, no one can prove who threw the stones. They said so themselves, according to that rag you're reading."

Anton purses his lips. "No more demos for me. If my mother found out it would kill her."

I'm surprised that Anton is so scared. He's strongly built, someone who never backs down in an argument. Once he showed up on campus with bruises to his face, blithely saying he fell over at soccer practice, but we all knew that he had been mugged by "poofta bashers" while he was on the prowl in a local park near campus at night time.

Sitting looking at him, I know that he won't change his mind about the Bluestone demonstration. I'm about to point out that Mona Lippi's injuries are collateral damage to the Cause, but I let it drop. Waste of breath.

"I thought you said Rita was coming," I say, to fill in the gap.

"She'll be here in a few minutes. I told her three thirty," Anton says.

A couple of minutes later Rita turns up, dressed in shorts and a red silk blouse. Her long black hair is massed on her shoulders, and she gives a big smile when she sees us and walks over to our table.

"Hi, you two. What are you up to?" she says.

Anton has folded the newspaper so that the Mona Lippi article isn't visible, and says, "Just chatting with Bozo here, and hoping you'd turn up to make it more interesting," he smiles. For some reason I feel embarrassed, not wanting Rita to find out about me throwing stones at the Bluestone Corporation building.

"Nice friend you've got," Rita says to me, and orders a cappuccino. "Be warned, the man cannot be trusted."

"I know," I stammer, and see Anton grinning out of the corner of my eye.

"What's wrong?" Rita asks.

"Nothing really," Anton says casually. "We're just mulling over yesterday's demo. Some idiot threw stones at the building we were picketing, caused some damage. It all seems a bit hairy."

"Yeah, that's right," I mutter.

"Oh," Rita says. "Sounds dangerous."

"Yeah," I say meekly.

We chat for a while, then Rita's cappuccino arrives, and Anton stands up and says he has to go.

"Got an essay to finish off for Monday," he says blithely, and makes a smooth exit. Anton can talk his way into and out of any situation, while people like me are blathering some unlikely excuse, red-faced and nonplussed.

"He's in a funny mood," Rita says, watching Anton leave, then turning her big brown eyes my way.

"Worried about the demonstrations, I think. Looks like he'll pull out of them."

"What about you? Are you pulling out?"

"Probably. It's mostly pretty boring." It seems like she hasn't seen the newspaper article about Mona Lippi, not yet anyway, so that gives me a bit of room to duck the issue as we chat on.

We establish that while I'm a Rolling Stones fan, she prefers the Beatles, we agree that Prime Minister Billy McMahon is a total idiot, and she tells me that if I'm conscripted for the Vietnam War, I should try to get off as a conscientious objector. Rita is easy company, and I gradually relax.

***

At the start of second term I'm in Poynton's Pub opposite the Royal Women's Hospital in Grattan Street, sitting at my favourite corner table waiting for Anton, who is running late for lunch.

With no warning a thin suave looking man sits down next to me and parks his beer on a coaster. He's faintly familiar; sandy hair, thirty-ish, nice suit, a tad self important.

"Harry Mott! Glad I've finally caught up with you," he says brightly, in an academic tone of voice. Definitely one of the "as it were" brigade, with first class honours in total bullshit.

"Sorry, don't think we've met."

"My name's Neil Bautervich. I've seen you around the place, thought I'd say hello."

"What's on your mind?" I say to this Neil Bautervich.

"Got a message for you."

"Who from?"

"Mutual friends."

"I don't know you, so I can't see how that would work."

"Not so. There are people who want to do you a favour, important people."

"Thank god for that," I say. "Someone cares after all."

"Ah, I thought you'd be an amusing sort of person. No, it's an important message, about your future."

"Like I said, who from?"

"I'm a journalist," he says. "And in the course of my work I meet all sorts of people. Some of them are in the security services, let us call them."

"OK," I say, with a sinking feeling. My boredom evaporates suddenly, and I feel the urge to run for it.

"And these people," Bautervich goes on, "think that you might be headed for some trouble over your actions at the recent violent demonstration against Bluestone Corporation."

"Ah," I say, trying to look unimpressed.

"Yes, ah! The message is that you might be in danger of losing your scholarship, unless you agree to certain terms."

"It's not illegal to demonstrate."

Anger rises in my throat, and I feel like punching him in the face, but I want to find out what the hell he's on about.

"No, it isn't illegal to demonstrate," he says. "But it is illegal to throw stones at a building and injure someone. Mona Lippi, the young lady in question, is quite willing to press charges."

"The police can't prove anything. There were heaps of people there. Why me?"

"Simple. Your mates in Revolutionary Student Action have dobbed you in. They reckon," Bautervich says, pausing to sip his beer, "that it was you who threw those stones, the ones that hit Mona Lippi in the face and injured her. Your revolutionary comrades aren't exactly sticking up for you."

"Bullshit." I want to sound dismissive, but I don't feel it, and Bautervich doesn't look convinced. It isn't too hard to imagine being dropped in it by my revolutionary comrades, as he calls them, for the good of the Cause, or more specifically to save the skins of the members of the inner circle. Namely Melissa Frankel and Sam Newbold.

"And?" I ask.

"My friends have a proposition for you," he says. "They would appreciate some inside information every now and then. In which case, we can guarantee that the charges are dropped, and you'll be able to finish your studies, graduate, and get on with your life."

"What information do you want?"

"When and where your little mates are going to meet. We're particularly interested in Sam Newbold. In Sam Newbold's case, we want to know when he's speaking in public next. He's their mouthpiece, a real troublemaker."

"And if I don't?"

"You'll be out on your ear in no time flat. Your scholarship shut down, banished from the university."

Bautervich sits back with a smug look on his face, and downs the rest of his beer.

"Harry, you're not worried about dobbing your mates in, are you?" he says. "You know that Revolutionary Student Action is just a Maoist front. Linked to the Maoist Communist Party in

Melbourne. And surely you've heard about Chairman Mao killing millions of his own people? You can't seriously believe in Maoism. Or want to protect people who do. A bright lad like you."

I glare at him while he passes over a slip of paper with a telephone number on it.

"Ring me every week, Monday midday, at this number," he says. "Starting next week. If I don't hear from you then, expect the worst."

"How do I know this is for real?" I say. "Maybe you're some nutcase trying to pull something on me."

"Don't worry, Harry," he says. "You're in good company. You'd be amazed at how many informers there are on campus. And a good job too, serving their country."

Neil stands up and looks down at me. "I've enjoyed our little chat. And by the way, since you didn't ask, Mona Lippi is still on sick leave. She's a lawyer, you know. She was looking forward to a bright career. Let's hope she'll be all right."

He smiles, saying as he heads off, "Have a nice lunch."

It hasn't taken me long to get into this mess. I've only just arrived at university, and here I am in more hot water than I can ever have imagined.

PART TWO
THE GOLDEN DRAGON

CHAPTER 5

SYLVIA

Eight years after she started work at Star Finance, Sylvia was nominated "Most Promising Female Executive of the Year" at the Annual Awards for Business Excellence in Melbourne. It was a stunning rise up the corporate ladder, and she owed it to Sam Newbold's recommendation of her when she first applied for a routine admin job she was barely qualified for.

Sylvia didn't see much of Sam these days. Their affair fizzled out shortly after she started work at Star Finance, Sam distracted by his third divorce and a raft of political setbacks in the Party.

She had been handed the Business Excellence award by Zelda Freestone, the only female mining magnate in the history of Australia, who congratulated her with a tight smile and the words, "Well done, my dear," shaking hands with her stubby fingers encrusted with diamond rings. Zelda introduced Freddie Wu to her briefly and left immediately, an abrupt person in everything she did.

Sylvia was intrigued by Freddie, from the way he could dominate a room full of people without having to say very much at all, to his encyclopedic knowledge of everything to do with business and politics. He was all charm, so that everyone seemed to defer to him before they even knew that he was a wealthy businessman and a member of China's elite. It was clear to Sylvia that Freddie Wu would be an even more powerful patron than Sam Newbold, and their relationship developed quickly.

Although Sylvia stood a head taller than Freddie, he was undeterred by her physical strength, even in bed. She had met an equal, and it was stimulating.

"You are a formidable young woman," he said a few weeks later as they were sitting in the back seat of Freddie's Volvo. It was an understated drive for someone so wealthy, although he did have a chauffeur, a silent man named Fong, with solid shoulders and a crewcut. "Vice President of Star Finance by the age of thirty. Excellent. You must meet more of the right people to help you in your career."

"I owe Star Finance a lot," she said. "And I'm very well paid in my current job."

"A business career is not only about money," Freddie said. "Real power is a rare commodity."

"What are you suggesting?"

"There are many possibilities," Freddie said. "I can introduce you to very influential people."

"What influential people? People like Zelda Freestone?"

Freddie smiled. "I like your frankness," he said. "Zelda is a good friend of mine, but not given to mentoring the next generation. We could begin with an introduction to someone like Michael Fontaine."

The name rang a bell, but Sylvia couldn't place him.

"Who's that?"

"Well, Michael heads up GoodLord Inc. An evangelical congregation, with many thousands of enthusiastic followers."

"A congregation?"

"Yes."

"Why would I be interested in meeting an evangelist?"

"A good question. Michael has the capacity to go very far indeed. His rise has been meteoric. He has a TV show, and soon he will command the loyalty of millions of followers. He might better be regarded as a rising star in the media."

"How does that translate into the real power you are talking about?"

"I think that you will find meeting him very useful."

It was difficult to work out what Freddie's line of business actually was, but of course when it came to real money, anything was possible.

***

The introduction to Michael Fontaine was low key. Freddie Wu hosted a charity function at an expensive hotel, ostensibly in aid of disadvantaged children, but clearly designed to provide a pleasant social occasion with networking opportunities for people who had a lot of money, and wanted more.

Without Freddie at her side, Sylvia would have been at the bottom of the pecking order in this room full of wealthy gladhanders who knew each other by their first names. Those who didn't have this advantage drifted to the periphery of the room like debris dispersed in the wake of a luxury yacht, faking important calls on their mobile phones while hoping for introductions to the rich and famous.

Sylvia, however, was guided into the spotlight. After a series of introductions to politicians, businessmen, TV celebrities, a media mogul, the owner of a ski resort, and various society hostesses, Freddie finally introduced her to Michael Fontaine.

He was an imposing middle aged man, with wavy blonde hair, a big smile and a booming voice.

"Hello again, Michael," Freddie said, steering Sylvia by the elbow so that she stood next to Fontaine. Freddie introduced the people around Fontaine, including his wife Isobel. She was a plump attractive woman in middle age who smiled brightly at Sylvia for a moment, before directing her smile back to Freddie and Fontaine.

Sylvia stood silently listening to Freddie and Michael Fontaine talking about Federal politics, then felt Isobel's hand on her arm.

"Are you interested in politics, Ms Rojo?"

"Not at all," Sylvia said. "Although politicians can be very interesting."

"Yes, we have several prominent politicians who have joined with us at GoodLord," Isobel said. "Have you considered joining GoodLord yourself?"

"No, I haven't," Sylvia said. "But Freddie speaks highly of it."

"Yes, Freddie is one of our major supporters. A very important businessman. And very generous."

Isobel wrinkled her nose, as though repressing more comments, then added, "You must join us. You will find it very enlightening."

"Yes, I'm sure I would," Sylvia responded. Isobel had a keen sense of her own importance, she decided, and obviously kept a watchful eye on young women who appeared on the horizon of her domain.

"Oh, good," Isobel smiled, and turned to her husband and Freddie, smoothly interrupting them. "Michael, Ms Rojo is going to join GoodLord," she said.

"Excellent!" Fontaine said, beaming at Sylvia.

"Sylvia is a very talented young woman," Freddie said, looking in turn at Fontaine and Isobel. "In fact, Sylvia has played a key role in the success of Star Finance."

"Has she now?" Fontaine was looking at Sylvia keenly.

"I've learned a great deal at Star Finance," Sylvia said. "I owe them a lot."

"As it happens, Michael, I was going to suggest to you, and to Isobel, that Sylvia would make an excellent executive in GoodLord," said Freddie.

"Wonderful," Fontaine said, as Isobel returned to his side.

"I'm sure Star Finance would understand if you took the next step in your career into a larger organization," Freddie smiled at Sylvia.

"Well, Sylvia, perhaps you would like to attend our Sunday Gathering this weekend, and have a chat afterwards?" Fontaine said.

"Certainly," Sylvia said.

"A great idea," said Freddie.

"That's settled then," Michael Fontaine said, and shook hands as Freddie led her away to meet a woman who looked like one of the lesser known TV newsreaders, but turned out to be the CEO of A Better Life, the charity they were supporting with donations from the proceeds of Freddie's event.

***

When she arrived at the GoodLord Sunday Gathering, Sylvia was expecting Southern USA barnstorming evangelism, like the TV shows, with a comical mix of syrupy pop songs about Jesus, peppered with bible readings and crass appeals for donations.

Freddie Wu had briefed her on GoodLord Inc, its key players, modus operandi and organizational structure in a chatty conversational style, but with all the fine detail of a military operation. However, he said little about Michael Fontaine's approach to preaching, apart from insisting that GoodLord was ushering in a paradigm shift in the entertainment media, and was not merely a new church experiencing phenomenal growth.

"I'm encouraging Michael to enter politics," Fredde said. "He has the gift of charisma, a TV show watched by millions, and great leadership qualities."

It all seemed like a bizarre notion to Sylvia, and her lack of interest in religion led her to dread the couple of hours of tedium she was expecting.

However, Michael Fontaine's preaching on the stage of the vast auditorium came as a pleasant relief. His booming voice was conversational and confiding, a cheerful antidote to the frustrations of a busy week at work, raising the kids, going to school and all the rest of it. Despite a lot of references to the Lord Jesus, and a mix of prayers and religious songs, the whole event was upbeat, a good natured variety show with intervals of harmless pop music, and biblical storytelling with a twist of self improvement.

Fontaine was an inspired speaker, no doubt about it, telling the vast audience of laughing and talking GoodLord devotees to enjoy their lives in the name of the Lord.

"Jesus looks after all of us, sinners included," he said with a broad smile, "and the Lord God himself wants us to be happy and prosperous!"

He looked around the huge auditorium, a figure of reassurance, blonde hair glinting under the spotlights.

"Yes, we are all sinners. But remember that Jesus died on the cross for us all, to save us from our sins!"

Cries of assent went up from the crowd, "Yes, He did!"

Fontaine ended with a parable about the love of Jesus for children, and then the band struck up again with another cheerful pop song, which sounded like it was based on the Bible story in which Jesus said something like, "Suffer little children to come unto me," something Sylvia remembered vaguely from Sunday School, but never understood as a child, and still didn't.

It certainly made a change from the gloom and doom of Sylvia's potted experience of the various Protestant churches that Mother took her to with Naomi and Jack when they were children. Solemn services in various little rundown churches as they moved from one shop to another in the bayside suburbs. All sin and suffering, gloomy music, solemn ministers delivering dreary sermons full of torpid clichés, everyone in their drab Sunday best.

Michael Fontaine, on the other hand, sang along in a pleasant baritone to the pop music delivered by the young band of musicians supported by a chorus of kids dressed in jeans and tee shirts, dancing and singing, all smiles and happy faces. The audience sang along as well, many of the young ones dancing in the aisles. In fact, a feature of the show was how many young people attended, all of them having a good time, rather than sitting stiff and silent in a church pew, only there because their parents brought them.

The diversity of the congregation was striking too, young and old, Anglo and Asian, Middle Eastern, what-have-you. On her way through the car park she had seen a range of vehicles, from scratched old Holdens to new European brands, and inside what was obviously a converted warehouse the audience reflected this range of wealth and hard-scrabble.

Sylvia hummed to the music and took the storytelling in her stride, much like a doting parent at a primary school parents' night. It had all the feelgood sense of a variety show, so long as you ignored the gauche moments of kitsch.

Afterwards Sylvia went backstage and found Fontaine surrounded by his acolytes, as Isobel greeted her and shepherded her inside a spacious office and offered her a seat and a cup of coffee. Isobel was wearing a billowing floral dress, in contrast to Sylvia's smart business pantsuit, and looked the part of a motherly volunteer at a local fete.

Isobel made a show of extracting a file from a filing cabinet, while a young girl that Sylvia recognized as a backing singer on stage brought in the coffee.

Fontaine entered, and extended his hand with a huge smile.

"Welcome, Sylvia, welcome. Great to see you, thank you for coming."

He asked how she found the Gathering, and Sylvia answered truthfully enough that she had enjoyed it. If she was going to follow Freddie's advice and progress her career with GoodLord, then at least the sort of show she had just witnessed was less painful than most of the work-related events she had endured in the last few years.

Sylvia wondered what the other managers were like, but going on what she had seen so far, the only problem would probably be Isobel, who minded Fontaine like the obsessed mother of a child movie star afraid of her charge being poached by Hollywood agents. At a guess, GoodLord was growing at a rate incomprehensible to someone like Isobel.

"Let's sit down and chat, Sylvia. We'd love to hear more about you."

"Certainly," Sylvia smiled, "and I'd love to hear more about you and GoodLord."

"Of course," Fontaine said, glancing at Isobel.

"I have an employee application form here in the file, Michael," Isobel said.

"Yes, dear," Fontaine said. "I think we can dispense with that for the moment. At Sylvia's level, I think that we need to consider these talks confidential, and explore the possibilities in the context of the Great Leap Forward we are about to undertake."

"Yes, of course," Isobel said.

"Great Leap Forward?" Sylvia asked.

"Just our little joke," Fontaine said. "We are contemplating major changes to cope with the huge growth in numbers we are experiencing. I understand that your recent work at Star Finance has included dealing with growth issues?"

"Yes, Star Finance expanded very quickly, opening offices right across the country to deal with rapid growth in its customer base. But I'm not sure how that would compare with your situation."

"Well, yes, it's probably unique. But Freddie tells me that you are a natural organizer, with a great strategic sense, which is what we need."

"That's good to hear. I have to tell you though, that I'm very happy with Star Finance. And to be honest, I'm only here because Freddie suggested it would be a good idea to hear what you have to say."

"Freddie has been a great help in setting down a few ideas," Fontaine said, and nodded at Isobel. She produced a typewritten couple of pages, which she handed over to Sylvia.

It was typical Freddie, a succinct summary of what was required, crafted to match Sylvia's résumé. It mentioned the need to offer an "industry standard" of pay for the position, with a salary range that made Sylvia smile to herself.

"Yes, that makes very real sense," she said to Fontaine. Isobel had more or less retired from the conversation at this point, and when Fontaine offered Sylvia the job, and she accepted, Isobel simply nodded along with Fontaine's welcome to her new start at GoodLord, starting in a month's time.

***

Michael Fontaine certainly had the gift when it came to shepherding a vast flock of worshipping admirers. It wasn't clear to Sylvia who they worshipped most; God or Michael Fontaine. Either way, membership continued to skyrocket, the Sunday Gatherings were growing nationwide, and donations kept flooding in.

The GoodLord Inc TV programs kept climbing up the ratings, with production values improved by hiring a professional media company at enormous expense.

However, when Sylvia began work at GoodLord she found a makeshift sort of organization. Planning was ad hoc, and the marketing budget seemed to have a life of its own, with large chunks of expenditure allocated willy-nilly to a variety of activities that made no sense.

Isobel Fontaine's office administration was adequate so far as it went, which was a basic computer accounting system and a set of incomplete personnel files. There were three "office girls," mainly handling membership and event management, pretty efficiently (all things considered), and there was someone in charge of the band and the singers, most of them enthusiastic amateurs, also quite good (all things considered).

Despite GoodLord's growing congregation and Michael's increasing popularity, it was obvious that there was a lot of wasted effort going into ad hoc public appearances, mostly on the whim of a celebrity evangelist having the time of his life. As Sylvia saw it, focus was the main priority. It should be possible to do twice as much with half the effort.

Rather than interviewing staff and ploughing through this mess under her own steam, Sylvia hired a consultant, with two assistants to do the donkey work for her. Charlotte Hung was appointed, recommended, of course, by Freddie Wu.

Charlotte was cheerful and competent, and minded her own business. She had little need of moral support, and mowed through the company finances like some high-tech vacuum cleaner, politely tossing out inefficient systems and replacing them with the latest software, and reassigning funds after brief discussions with Sylvia. They saw eye to eye on what needed to be done, and progress was swift.

Charlotte Hung's attack on the bloated and misdirected marketing budget was a classic operation in ruthless, logical reorganization. The two young males assisting her were models of efficiency, with all the keen instincts of natural auditors. They arrived at the office early every morning, and left late, spending all day slaving away at their computers, chatting into their mobile phones, working their way methodically through every office in the building.

On the one hand, no one was ever personally accused of slackness or inefficiency, let alone fraud and corruption. On the other, their basic assumption within the team was that the natural order of things dictated that at best, most people were lazy and self-serving, and at worst dishonest or even criminal, and swift action was needed to fix it.

"Marketing in particular needs a new start," Charlotte said to Sylvia. "It lacks direction, there is no real plan."

"Yes, I agree," Sylvia said, and approved a total overhaul of the marketing budget, with a review of the marketing department to reassess priorities.

The marketing manager was beside himself at these changes. A large fat man, sweating and anxious, he stormed into Sylvia's office and demanded the return of funds cut from his budget.

"This is outrageous!" he protested. "There is no justification for these cuts!"

"I note your objections," Sylvia said. "But the review stands," and she went ahead with a swift dismissal process that saw him replaced within weeks.

Michael Fontaine's public appearances also needed streamlining, so Sylvia hired Anna Kalajian, by all accounts a savvy public relations operator. She seemed like a good fit to Sylvia, young and smart, and attractive enough to prevail upon Michael when it came to knocking some sense into his schedule.

This change required nudging Isobel into more of a pastoral care role with GoodLord's growing staff, something that Sylvia put a gloss on by creating a new Human Resources department for Isobel to lord over. This kept her out of the way when it came to day-to-day management of Fontaine's schedule.

Fontaine's increasing fame had led to any number of invitations to public events, not only from the rich and famous who now belonged to GoodLord, but also a welter of community events, from school fêtes to bowling club anniversaries and various charities.

"Your good works need huge resources to be really effective, Michael," Sylvia said. "I know that it is tempting to try to help everyone, but you can help more people by attending fewer, but bigger events. We need support from influential people."

However, Michael had continued to be an easy target for any invitation that came his way.

"We need to focus Michael on the big stuff, I'm sure you understand," Sylvia said to Anna.

"No problem," Anna said. "I'll draw up a list of publicity targets and prominent supporters."

Sylvia didn't need to coach Anna in what was important, and what was not. Fontaine's appearances at the big end of town increased tenfold over a matter of months, whereas insignificant appointments dwindled away to nothing, and his public profile grew exponentially.

Sylvia found it interesting to observe the effects of Michael's growing fame. His adoring fans were rapt in his eloquence and breezy charm. He made them feel good, he understood them, he was an inspiration. And above all, he was a national celebrity.

Michael's security had to be increased on his outings in public, and it became obvious to Sylvia that Michael basked in the attention, and had gaps in his schedule when he was supposedly playing golf. Rather, she guessed, he was sneaking off to meet a female fan in private. This was not something she could expect Anna Kalajian to resolve. It was more than a scheduling issue.

After her affair with Sam Newbold, Sylvia knew that this sort of narcissism had no boundaries. The trick was to protect Michael from himself, vetting his secret affairs for signs of a media setup, and quietly easing the women involved out of the picture as he tired of them, with a combination of money and threats.

Everything was going to plan, and Sylvia increased her contact time with Michael, stroking his ego and making him feel that nothing was impossible.

After six months, with Freddie Wu dominating the Board with a few well chosen associates, Charlotte Hung in charge of finance, and Anna Kalajian managing Michael's public appearances, Sylvia was formally appointed CEO of a revitalized GoodLord Inc. The promotion came with a significant increase in pay, and entry to the world of high level CEOs clustered around town in a variety of exclusive networks. Much of the gratuitous advice she received from older male CEOs was patronizing and irrelevant, but on the other hand she discovered two or three female top executives who knew their stuff and offered useful insights.

GoodLord was streamlined, efficient, and making good use of its ever-increasing revenue. New interstate branches of GoodLord were being established with new pastors and administrative staff, and GoodLord was now a national phenomenon. It was time for the next stage of Sylvia's plan.

***

A major difference between Sylvia and Isobel was that Isobel didn't have enough imagination to understand Michael's potential. Sylvia had big plans for Michael, whether he knew it or not.

They increasingly confided in each other over big and small decisions, with Michael reading his sermons to her and Sylvia giving him feedback and advice, despite her complete ignorance of all things religious.

Michael, however, had stupendous knowledge of the Bible. He could quote chunks of it from memory, and at this stage of his career he also had a stock of themes for speeches on hand that he could tap into in a blink.

Sylvia became Fontaine's right-hand person, and as they had more time together they inevitably ended up in bed, grabbing an hour or two here and there in various apartments lent to her by Freddie Wu. Michael was anxious about keeping up appearances, afraid that Isobel would find out about them and raise hell. On top of that, a preacher who wants to be a politician had to protect his reputation, he explained to Sylvia, who tried not to laugh.

What was needed in this situation was longer term planning, to ensure they had more time alone together. Sylvia made careful preparations before their first clandestine weekend away, consulting with Freddie Wu about the security aspects of her plans, given Michael's high level of public recognition and the media interest in every move he made.

"I would like to take Michael somewhere secluded, for the weekend, so he can get away from it all, and we can have time to discuss the future at leisure," Sylvia said to Freddie. "I can trust Anna Kalajian to manage the office side of it, but I still need a high level of security throughout the weekend. And I need some solid excuse to cover Michael's absence for a weekend."

"No problem at all," Freddie said. "I have access to a number of secluded country houses, including a house by the sea, on its own large property, or a retreat in the mountains, perhaps?"

"Tell me about the house near the sea."

"It's a large, secluded house on the Mornington Peninsula, surrounded by several acres of land, with private entry. And close to the beach. It has state of the art security, and an adjoining cottage which we use for our security teams."

"Security teams?"

"Yes. I suggest you use one of my teams. Then you'll have total confidentiality, no leaks to the media or anyone else."

"Excellent," Sylvia said. "Any ideas on excuses for Michael going off for a weekend?"

"It might be simpler to send Isobel off somewhere. Perhaps a glamorous conference in a nice location? I'll have that checked out, and get back to you."

A few days later Freddie confirmed that there was an evangelical conference coming up soon in Hawaii, and that he could wangle an invitation for Isobel to speak on the topic of the challenges for female leaders to the evangelical women's international group.

"Perfect," Sylvia said.

Isobel was delighted to receive a prestigious invitation from Evangelical Mothers of America to speak at the Hawaii conference, but was clearly nervous about the overseas travel and making a speech to a large crowd at a conference. Sylvia assigned Anna Kalajian as a supporting colleague, wangling her a ticket to go with Isobel to Hawaii, and help her prepare her speech. The conference topics were the usual melange of pop psychology and feel-good self congratulation, and when Sylvia read the draft that Anna showed her she felt that Isobel would be a good fit into that environment.

"Have a great trip," she said to Isobel when she farewelled her. "I know you'll do GoodLord proud."

"I will, I will," Isobel said, obviously chuffed, but at the same time totally daunted.

***

When Sylvia suggested a weekend together, Michael smiled.

"Great idea!" he said. "But how could we arrange that?"

"Isobel's trip will allow us some time together, if that suits you."

"Yes, yes," Michael mumbled, obviously embarrassed, but pleased as well.

"I understand that it's a little risky for you. But don't worry, I can arrange a totally secluded location for us, by a private beach on the Mornington Peninsula. And I've hired a security team aside from our usual arrangements to make sure we are not disturbed."

It all worked perfectly. The house was prepared, the security team was in place, and the official bushfire danger warnings for the area were on "low".

Freddie sent a driver to pick them up in an anonymous but powerful and comfortable black SUV with privacy screened windows. The driver was an affable Scot called Alex, large, middle-aged and very discreet in his manner. Ex-military, Freddie said, whatever that meant. The SUV was fitted with a glass screen that popped up between them and the driver, allowing them the freedom of a private chat on the way down, and with a drinks cabinet and their choice of a large range of music on the sound system.

They cleared the city in cold clear sunshine, just beating the afternoon peak hour traffic, a southerly breeze promising rain over the weekend.

On the last leg of the trip they navigated a rough country road in perfect comfort as darkness fell, entered the property through an anonymous unmarked gap in a very large cypress hedge, and followed a gravel road for several hundred metres along a downhill slope between tall pine trees. As they approached the house they could hear waves crashing down at the beach, and they finally arrived at the front door of a double-storey mansion with well-lit front steps and a thick wooden door.

"I imagine this is what Chequers might be like when the British PM scoots off for a country weekend," Michael laughed. "Polo in the morning, and lunch invitations for the President of France."

"Don't get your hopes up. It'll be buttered toast for breakfast and vegemite sandwiches for lunch," Sylvia said.

It was obvious that she was joking when Michael opened the fridge once they were inside, discovering all sorts of delicacies, and expensive bottles of wine on the kitchen table.

"Very impressive," Michael said, walking around the ground floor rooms, all large, comfortable, and superbly furnished.

With the heaters on at full blast to dispel the cold night air, they relaxed in front of the TV, following a viewing of the Friday night sports roundup with some idiotic drama about a retired pastor who discovers crop circles made by aliens, which Michael seemed to enjoy as Sylvia resigned herself to making sure that he was relaxed and happy. At least she had his full attention, unlike their first brief surreptitious encounters. Phone calls from Isobel could be managed easily given the difference in time zones, and Isobel's busy schedule at the conference. They were able to relax together for the first time, with no need for the hurried meetups they had managed so far.

Later, in bed, taking their time, Sylvia grudgingly admitted to herself that while Michael could not of course be compared with Charlie Triado, Sam Newbold, or Freddie Wu, he did at least make a good showing for someone at his age and level of unfitness.

"Not bad for a fat old preacher," she might have said afterwards, but confined herself to a show of gentle admiration for his prowess, and stroked his ego enough to guarantee both of them a good night's sleep.

They spent a bracing hour on the beach below the house in a cool breeze the next morning, and spent the rest of the day lazing about as they drank the wine provided for them.

The property was called "Xanadu," despite it being one of those modern box-like concrete affairs, with a view of the dark grey ocean across tea-tree scrub and rolling storm clouds mounting above them. It was too crisp and business-like a setting for such a romantic name, but it was certainly the ideal hideaway for long chats about the future of GoodLord, with Michael eager to talk about his brilliant career, and the wonderful prospects for a couple so much in love after finding each other against all the odds, a development so rapid that Sylvia had to smile.

Alex, the driver, turned out to be a superb chef. He was silent but amiable, and light on his feet for such a large man, a comfortable presence in the background in his downstairs quarters next to the garage.

The whole house was connected to the security cameras, except for their suite upstairs, they were assured, and the outside sentries flitted about, dim silhouettes only to be seen out of the corner of an eye.

This way Sylvia at least knew where Michael was, safe and sound, while advancing her own agenda more quickly than she had thought possible as she led him gently through her view of the future in those intimate moments when she had his full attention.

Michael could not have been more malleable, like a puppy looking for its next treat when it obeys the command to "sit" before crossing the road at a traffic light.

***

Keeping Isobel Fontaine busy when she returned from Hawaii was a priority, and Sylvia arranged a new prestigious position for her, a Vice President position that included member welfare and the welcoming function.

When Isobel went on stage to preside at her first monthly ceremony as Vice President Welcomes, Sylvia watched from the sidelines backstage, waiting for the little white pills she had slipped into Isobel's coffee to take effect. She could see that Isobel was nervous, although at first she managed to keep up appearances, helped by the cheering and clapping from the audience.

"It's a very real pleasure to welcome new members to GoodLord," she said. "A growing congregation means GoodLord can reach out to more and more people, spreading the good news of the gospel. Every single member counts at GoodLord, all of you are a credit to our crusade."

After a few minutes, though, Isobel began to falter, her speech slurring, her hand knocking against the microphone as she dropped the speech notes she was holding. She bumbled along for a minute or two, then attempted to pick up her notes, but as she leaned down she fell face first onto the floor of the stage, so that Anna Kalajian ran to her aid.

Anna held Isobel by an elbow, trying to help her up, only to have her boss tumble backwards, legs in the air, and fall flat on her back. Various people on the sidelines scrambled to help her, and the band director quickly responded with a musical break as Isobel was helped from the stage, red-faced and flustered, trying to rearrange her clothing as she disappeared from view.

Sylvia was impressed that once Isobel was taken care of, Anna was able to take over her role, approaching the microphone confidently, apologizing briefly for the delay with a few words to reassure the audience that Isobel was being taken care of after experiencing a severe migraine, and carrying on in great style.

"I'm sure that Isobel didn't have a drink before she went on," Sylvia said to Michael afterwards. "Is her health OK?"

"She's being checked by the doctors, but they don't seem to think anything is terribly wrong. Perhaps she was simply overcome by the occasion. She's always been a little bit shy."

"That's a shame," Sylvia said. "I must say, though, that I was impressed by Anna's competence after Isobel collapsed. Perhaps we should put her in charge of Welcomes until Isobel has recovered?"

Michael agreed, and Sylvia could see that it would be an easy transition from Isobel's Welcoming role, to a permanent replacement, preferably Anna Kalajian.

Isobel's recovery became delayed as she grew increasingly reliant on alcohol and pills. Finally she was placed in a nursing home, protected from hurting herself, safe from the prying eyes of reporters for the tabloid newspapers.

"I don't know what happened to poor Isobel," Michael groaned. "She's not the woman she once was. It's no use visiting her any more, she barely knows who I am."

"These things happen, Michael," Sylvia said.

It was annoying that Michael was still looking in the rear view mirror, but on the other hand, his dependence on Isobel until Sylvia arrived meant that there was a gap in his life that needed to be filled.

CHAPTER 6

HARRY

The morning after my meeting with Melissa Frankel I sit in my office mulling over what I now know about Sam Newbold's past history. By this time I've spent weeks fossicking around in his past like a seagull scavenging for tidbits in a rubbish tip. Questioning Sam's former colleagues over a quiet beer, reading piles of documents and newspaper clippings, raiding the Party archives. His life is the usual politician's mess of bloated self interest and relentless ambition, coupled with a trail of wreckage in his personal and political relationships. However, while there's a lot of drama, there are no hanging offences.

None of this matters now that Melissa Frankel has accused Sam Newbold of being a police spy. On the record, albeit in secret. At last I am getting somewhere.

The context here is that more than twenty years after the end of the Vietnam War every man and his dog who was involved in student radical politics in the sixties and seventies is still arguing in newsletters, journals, forums and conferences, and more recently on the internet, about who did what during the struggle against the Vietnam War. Who had the correct political line, who the traitors were, who the heroes, who the leaders. They all furiously curate their résumés in these verbal brawls, producing alibis and excuses as though they're on trial in court.

For the small minority of students who were involved in demonstrations, this battle for radical glory on the Left is still endlessly and bitterly fought, as vitriolic as it was decades ago, even as more recent generations of aspiring politicians arrive on the scene and have no idea what the hell the old guard are talking about.

It's a similar battle on the Right, of course, except that the conservatives are less trendy, and generally not as photogenic. Both sides are so full of vehement certainty and moral outrage, for the duration of their whole lives, it seems, they could be mistaken for religious fanatics.

Some of the student politicians from back in the day have risen to high rank in the mainstream parties in recent times, their actions back then a badge of honour in their careers.

Amidst all this shouting and posturing, the revelation that Sam Newbold, one of the key players in the student anti Vietnam War movement in Australia, was a police spy, would be like a hand grenade thrown into a crowded bus.

***

Fears of surveillance by the anti Vietnam War protestors were validated by one interesting detail I come across in my searches in the National Archives; a Special Branch report about a Revolutionary Student Action meeting held soon after the Bluestone demonstration:

Special Branch
SECRET
VICTORIA
BRANCH COPY
No. 0987/72
102 AMY STREET, CARLTON
DATE: 23 JUNE, 1972

1. *The following university students are currently residing at 102 Amy Street, Carlton:*
Sam NEWBOLD (VPP 19051)
Melissa FRANKEL (VPP 18816)
Clive (fnu)
At least half a dozen others attended the meeting of the student Maoist group on the above date.

2. *Because they are apprehensive about phone taps, the house does not have a telephone line. Lookouts are posted when meetings are held, and the inhabitants move between different 'safe houses' at irregular times.*

AGENT'S COMMENTS: *Frankel is clearly the leader of the Maoist group, and conducts strategy sessions for demonstrations and illegal activities at this address.*

The irony is, of course, that at the end of 1972, not long after this report was written, the anti-war movement stopped virtually overnight when Gough Whitlam was elected Prime Minister and Australian troops were withdrawn from Vietnam. Revolutionary Student Action and all the other activist groups disappeared, university campuses went back to sleep, and I had no more juicy information to report to Neil Bautervich.

It became clear to me that nothing radicalizes middle class students more than the threat of conscription into the army to fight in a distant, ugly war. And once conscription ended, so did dissent.

***

The next step is to report my findings to the big cheese in his shiny new office.

The elevator takes us past mid-level offices with their open-plan cubicles, dank little kitchens and photocopier corners, to the top of the building where Noah Kowalski, CEO of the Secretariat, rules over all and sundry.

According to Ben Reilly, my boss, the Secretariat is Noah's stamping ground, his power base, from where he can sally forth, like a warlord in medieval Mongolia, hunting down his enemies and spreading fear and confusion in the ranks. Noah Kowalski is Ben's new boss, and I'm here to report to him on the results of my investigation into Sam Newbold.

I sit with Ben on a leather couch with a view of Fitzroy Gardens, around the corner from the Trades Hall building where the unions hang out. And just down the road from the State Parliament. Ben is an old mate from university days when we lived in the same student share house in Carlton. He was finishing the final year of his honours degree in Political Science while I spent most of my time in Poynton's Pub, falling in love with Rita Kapernaros and running the risk of failing my first year of Economics. We're a classic example of old mates hiring old mates.

"Listen, Harry. Do you really believe Melissa Frankel's story? That Sam Newbold was a police spy?" Ben asks me yet again while we wait. He's sincere and earnest, tall and thin, with a beard and glasses, the stereotype of a committed progressive Labour man, and the most honest person I've ever known.

"Yep. It all rings true. The thing is, we need to use it before Melissa does."

"OK," Ben says, looking glum.

I don't think Ben likes all the skullduggery. Never did, never will, despite the fact that he has risen steadily in the murky world of state politics, due to his capacity to come up with crystal clear policies and sharply defined speeches complete with sound bites, all dredged from the dross served up in endless committee meetings. In his new job as chief of staff to a Labour Party bigwig like Noah Kowalski he can report Melissa's revelations about Sam Newbold to the top of the heap.

Ben is a policy wonk, a big-picture man concerned with the future direction of the Party. My role is the deeply satisfying one of the investigator who rakes in the dirt that destroys reputations in the wars between political factions. An odd match, but a good one. And longer term, it is the Sam Newbold investigation that will bring me into Noah Kowalski's orbit, working on special projects for him. A nice piece of luck, enough to consolidate a career as time passes and you wonder if you'll ever get anywhere.

A brisk, affable woman with a ponytail waves us into Noah's office, and we find him bent over his desk drawers.

"Thanks, Rochelle," Noah mutters to her, glancing in our direction as we stand waiting. "Where the hell is that folder," he says to himself. "Take a seat guys," he adds, and goes to the door, calling out, "Rochelle, could you bring that folder I was working on!"

Almost immediately she appears and hands him a green folder, and he flips through it.

"OK, let's get to it," he says, looking up. "How reliable is this stuff about Sam Newbold being a police spy back in the day?" He glances from one to the other of us, and Ben signals for me to answer.

"Melissa Frankel is a successful lawyer, as you may know, and has a strong reputation as a straight shooter. No bullshit."

"Yeah, I've seen her on TV," says Noah, trying to conceal his pleasure at this gold nugget hidden amongst the mullock, but it is obvious he is tickled pink.

Noah Kowalski and Sam Newbold are in different Labour factions, with Sam in an alliance of progressives in the parliamentary wing of the Party, and Noah tightly linked to powerful unions. They couldn't be more different, Noah with his pit bull approach to politics, and Sam, smooth as silk with his polite calm even when under fire from his opponents in debates on TV.

Any extra ammunition in this war is a huge bonus, and Noah is bitterly engaged in the fight to the death against the privatization of Government-owned enterprises that Sam Newbold supports. Bitter intrigue in a labyrinth of deep trenches in an unending war. Totally incomprehensible to outsiders.

"Well done, guys," Noah says, and leans back in his huge office chair glancing from one to the other of us, as we sit there soaking up the rare compliment.

Noah looks out of place seated at an imposing desk surmounted by what looks like a brand new computer, with papers and documents piled around him. He is rummaging in a desk drawer, and I can see that his fingers are stained with nicotine, and the nails bitten to the quick. A skinny little guy with a mop of black hair and bad teeth, he wears a rumpled suit carelessly, with a tie adrift at the collar, like someone after a big big night on the town.

Word is that he drives a battered orange Datsun filled with fast food wrappers and old betting slips. Apparently Noah is a heavy gambler, racehorses, games of footy, you name it. I can imagine him propped up on a stool at the local TAB, watching the races on the screen, betting big on rank outsiders.

Everything about his appearance shouts bogan, someone from a penniless background who has clawed his way up to a top job, living on his wits and his willingness to plunge a knife into an opponent's back.

In fact the backstory is that Noah lives with his obstetrician wife in a nice suburb, and has three kids in private schools, although I doubt that he has signed on in the local golf club.

While all this might be true enough, he is a ruthless bastard, no mistake, the prime toe-cutter in the Party, often referred to as "a nasty little shit" by his enemies. However, despite all the fear and loathing, his face is alive with energy and intelligence, and there is no doubt who is boss.

The accusation of Sam Newbold being a police spy has everything that Noah has been hoping for. All the other slurs and bits of gossip about Sam Newbold are merely the typical dirty laundry of any politician you can poke a stick at. Maybe some of the details about the low points of Sam's personal life can be worked up into an unpleasant passing controversy, but it would not amount to a coup de grâce. Multiple divorces and affairs and child support cases aren't that unusual in this line of work.

On the other hand, the accusation that Sam acted as a police spy against his student radical mates, all still alive and kicking, is sudden death for a politician, especially with the left wing of the party. He would be swept away by a shitstorm of outrage and abuse. It would make him a traitor to all that is glorious about the Aussie tradition of mateship, especially amongst politicians.

The blackmail of Sam Newbold works a treat. In the end, Sam gets the position of Leader of the Opposition for the Party in the State Government, but he is gently informed that he will need to toe the line once he is in the job, or get turfed out with a character assassination attack. After all, spying for the police is worse than fraud, rape, and quite possibly homicide. The one indiscretion that would ruin him for good. In this way, he will be in charge, but beholden to those in the know. In other words, held to ransom due to a dirty secret in his past. A situation which I guess applies to most politicians who get anywhere at all.

No one in this cage fight wants the hoo-ha of a public victory, so long as Sam Newbold is too hobbled to stray off the path marked out for him. Not just because that would avoid all the fuss, but because it also means that this nasty little secret can be held against Sam for the term of his natural life, keeping him offside at any time when he shows any signs of initiative.

They go to all this trouble, rather than seeking out an alternative leader, because Sam is their only hope of winning the next election, coming up fast. No one else even vaguely looks like a potential State Premier, such is the leaderless situation of the Party.

As for Ben, I think that he sees this behind-the-scenes stuff as an annoying distraction from the real business at hand, like the sudden eruption of a drunken brawl at a wedding reception. In Ben's opinion, yes, shit happens, but we should stay focused on the main game, stuff like developing sound policies for the next State Labour Government. Ben doesn't seem to grasp that for most people the drunken brawl is in fact the main game.

***

It will take a miracle to win the next State election, even with Sam Newbold as the new Leader of the Opposition. More needs to be done than just a change of leader, the whole party needs a major renovation, like an unloved weatherboard cottage that hasn't had a paint job in twenty years, suffering from dry rot from the ground up. There's a lot to be done, but if anyone can fix it, that's Noah Kowalski. Starting now.

And here I am again outside Noah's office at the Secretariat with Ben Reilly, about to be briefed by Noah on the Renewal Project, a last ditch attempt at getting the Party back into shape.

"The Renewal Project is designed to fix up the fucking mess we're in. The role of the Secretariat is to implement the project and deliver recommendations to the Party. And believe me, the time for renewal is long overdue. Your team, Ben, will play a lead role in implementation of the recommendations. One of our starting points will be to act on the recent Party polling. OK so far?"

"That's right," Ben says. "We've reviewed the poll findings, and we'll start the interview process for the new leadership positions as soon as you give the word."

"OK," Noah says. "We need to get a move on now. This is going to be the mother of all reorganization projects. I've lined up an office for the project a couple of floors down, with staff facilities, computers, photocopiers and so on. Plus my crew can give you any extra admin support you need, especially when it comes to networking across various areas. Get going immediately, and we'll meet again at the end of the week."

No messing around, with Noah. It's all systems go, and we start interviewing every staffer above the level of irrelevant.

The Renewal Project is all about winners and losers. You're either on the inside of what's happening, in which case you are looking forward to a promotion, or on the outside, in which case your career is over. It's a massive sorting process, like running sheep through a gate, this way to the Royal Show, or the other, to the abattoirs.

Nearly everyone I interview has been through reviews before, and assume that this is yet another one. Reviews are rites of passage for them, and they are like war veterans recounting battles lost and won. Except this review is far more drastic than most.

The end result is a bloodbath, a miniature French Revolution of bloodthirsty revolutionaries, imprisoned minor aristocrats, severed heads, destitute peasants and slaughtered bystanders.

Our final report, which Noah grinds through sentence by sentence before submitting it to the relevant committee, announces a "streamlined" Party headed up by newly anointed political heavies gifted new departments. Entire units are abolished and staff sidelined more or less indiscriminately. Noah's influence is set in stone, at least until he chooses to retire, at which point he will become a Grand Old Man of the Party, called upon for his opinion by up-and-coming numbers men in the next generation.

In amongst the mayhem, Ben Reilly has bestowed upon him the title of Executive Director Strategic Futures, a new research and consultancy outfit for the Party. My own role as a consultant achieves some added gloss in Ben's elevation to the higher realms of political bullshit.

"Excellent, gentlemen," Noah says when he first visits Ben's new office. Nowhere near as big as Noah's, of course, but a step up all the same. "A job well done."

His tone is sardonic, he's wearing a new suit, with a new haircut, and he looks like someone who has just backed the winner of the Melbourne Cup.

Unfortunately it turns out that all our efforts are irrelevant, and Sam Newbold is defeated in the State election by a large majority. Sam takes all the blame, so that everyone else, including Noah, can carry on regardless. Nonetheless, Labour is left behind the eight ball. Defeated, broke, and leaderless. The new Leader of the Opposition, a bland nonentity known for his ability to offend no one, is a stop-gap designed to give the factions time to regroup and fight it out again for their favoured candidates.

This result is the sort of stalemate that brings joy to the hearts of the new Coalition Government, since they now have a free ride on top of the usual honeymoon after an election, and can do pretty much what they please. Which means pork-barrelling to their heart's content, treating Treasury like their personal piggy bank with no fear of exposure, a free rein to pursue their favourite vendettas against their political opponents, and vanity projects up the gazoo in every Coalition electorate in the state. And in the meantime the Labour Opposition is bogged down fighting an internal war with no end in sight.

***

"Now that Labour has lost yet another State election," I say angrily, looking around the dinner table, "we are in for a real dose of all that free market crap from the Coalition."

My dinner companions are already looking uneasy, sensing a long rant on the way. Anton is closely inspecting his fingernails, while my hosts, Ben and Fiona, exchange a look that says "here we go". Only Rita looks neutral, which is ominous.

I can't mention Sam Newbold being blackmailed over the police spy accusation in front of our wives. Or in front of Anton, for that matter. But Ben knows what I'm on about.

"It's a bit more complicated than that," Ben says calmly. "Labour has some real issues to resolve."

"You mean, like what the hell does Labour really stand for now that it's run by BMW socialists?" I say. Ben tries to say something, but I keep going. "When is a market ever 'free', for fuck's sake? It's a fantasy! Free of what? Regulation? Monopolies? Tax perks? Juicy government contracts?"

I've had a few drinks, and now I'm really starting to rant. Ben is still looking at me pensively, Fiona is smiling her usual dreamy smile. She started the evening by talking passionately about refugees, Aboriginals and other lost causes, as if the powers that be were ever going to change any of that. Or the voters. Then she went on about how the Greens were the only party that cared about the environment and diversity, and how logging should be banned, when I cut her off. I don't know how anyone can vote for a party that wants to put timber workers out of a job, whole towns of them, and I told her so.

Fiona is one of those trendy middle class Greenies who likes the occasional joint, but is against drug use, and has an idealized view of life in the country, as though Australia is just one big park. And yet she's so nice, a truly kind person. I just don't get what she doesn't understand about it all.

"A few years after I graduated," I go on with my rant, "my economics degree was irrelevant. The whole bloody discipline shifted from worship of Keynes, to adoration of that godawful Milton Friedman. Guru of the free market."

"All academic disciplines follow the fashions," Anton says dismissively. "Anyway, economists have never had a clue what they're on about."

"Yeah, true," I say. "But in this case we're talking about changing all of society, not just an academic discipline. The working classes have always been disenfranchised, but now the middle classes have been welcomed to the world of bugger-all basic employment rights."

"In the end we're all better off without all the bureaucratic rules, especially around wages," Anton says. "Tradesmen can be their own boss, and everyone can negotiate their own pay. The unions are rigid and out of date. They won't last much longer."

"Well, there's a myth for you," I say. "The only people negotiating their own pay are the bosses, with huge bonuses. Bloody accountants are no better than economists."

"Don't you get a bonus?" Anton grins at me, and Ben laughs.

"Fuck off," I say, with impeccable logic.

Rita is staring at me bleakly, probably weighing up the possibility of an early end to the evening, if not to our marriage. Here I am amongst friends; my oldest friends, and my own dear wife, who puts up with me, I know not why, and this is how I repay them, boring them to death.

Finally Rita says, "Time to go home," to me, as if talking to a toddler with a soiled nappy.

Of course I don't argue with Rita. She's right, it's time to go.

Once we get home Rita says, "What the hell was all that about?" and goes straight to bed without waiting for an answer, while I spend an hour or so in the toilet, throwing up every few minutes until I feel I've been wrung dry.

When I wake up on the living room couch before dawn, stiff and cold, my mouth tasting like the bottom of a cockatoo's cage, it's as though nothing has changed since my drinking days as a student. Except that now I wake up in a nice house with my lovely wife snoring lightly in the bedroom. A definite improvement, I decide, and undress and get into bed alongside Rita, managing not to wake her up.

Hopefully all will be forgiven in the morning, but I'll probably have to work for it, maybe bring Rita breakfast in bed.

CHAPTER 7

SYLVIA

Once Michael's divorce went through, and a little time had passed, they announced their engagement to Sylvia's parents.

Luckily both Naomi and Jack were not invited to the first get-together to introduce Michael to Sylvia's parents, something she had to prevent when talking to her mother on the phone.

"Just the four of us, Mother," Sylvia insisted. "Let's keep it simple," she said. Or as simple as it could get, given Eileen's unfathomable prejudices against most of humanity.

"My mother has high standards," Sylvia had said bitterly to Michael as the day of their get-together approached. "No one comes up to scratch, except the people she is trying to impress, someone like the local mayor who happens to be a descendant of a convict who came to Australia with the First Fleet. As if that is any recommendation."

"No First Fleeters among my mob," Michael said cheerily.

"Nor mine," Sylvia said. "God knows why she carries on like this."

"We'll be fine," Michael said.

"Yes, I know. It's just that I have a hard time stopping myself from throttling her."

Michael laughed, but he only knew the half of it, of course.

Although Victor and Eileen Rojo knew who Michael was, Eileen couldn't decide whether to be overawed by his celebrity, or to look down her nose at a parvenu minister of the Pentecostal faith. By this time, Victor had become quite wealthy, with three successful supermarkets releasing them from their hardscrabble life. As a result of her growing social status as the wife of a successful businessman, Eileen was by now fully ensconced in the local Anglican church, counted the vicar as a "dear friend," and had donated a family pew, in the front section of the congregation.

Sylvia observed that Eileen compromised by being polite but aloof in Michael's presence, a form of noblesse oblige when a family member brings home someone whose provenance is not entirely beyond doubt.

Victor and Michael, on the other hand, got on like a house on fire, laughing and chatting about everything from Test cricket matches and the footy, to the general decline of politics and the need for common sense to prevail on all the usual issues of the day.

"He's an excellent bloke," Victor said to Sylvia, while Michael was chatting to Eileen. "No side on him at all."

Sylvia knew that Michael was capable of trying to talk Eileen into enlisting in GoodLord, and had specifically warned him against it.

"Going to church is purely about social mobility for Mother," she told him. "You can rely on your money to do the talking if you want to impress her."

"I gather you two don't get on," Michael laughed.

"She's ignored me and my sister since we were born. She only cares about Jack."

Despite the fact that an open wedding would have filled the MCG and attracted unprecedented publicity, Sylvia preferred to accept an offer of a confined private space in the gardens of Zelda Freestone's Portsea mansion. Their wedding was a private affair, both of them agreeing to keep it as small as possible, since after all it was the second marriage of an evangelical preacher with a large congregation to satisfy, and with a former wife in the wings, albeit one barely aware of her surroundings in a luxury nursing home that quietly dealt with severe cases of "mental illness," as it used to be called in the old days.

Zelda's property was heavily guarded, and access was blocked to the general public. The guest list was limited to a couple of hundred of their closest and most wealthy supporters, and a sprinkling of prominent politicians from the major parties.

A celebrity celebrant named Cynthia Snell officiated, a buxom blonde with an ingratiating manner who offered "a wedding to remember" to all her clients on her website, which was replete with photos of Cynthia and the bride and groom smiling broadly at the camera and gushing reviews recommending her creative talent in ensuring that your special day would be a huge success.

These arrangements brought a scowl to Eileen Rojo's face, although from Sylvia's point of view they were far better than her mother's demands for them to marry in her local church. How a Church of England vicar could be expected to conduct the wedding of a divorced evangelical preacher was a puzzle to Sylvia. She had to admit that Cynthia Snell's approach to weddings was more suited to some kind of TV reality show, but anything was preferable to a religious ceremony.

"Mother would complain no matter what we did," she said to Michael. "Imagine if we did have her scrawny little vicar do it, she would try to get total control over the whole thing."

Naomi and Jack came along to the ceremony and played their allotted roles reluctantly but creditably, Naomi with her wannabe artist husband, wealthy nephew of a former State Premier, and Jack still mysteriously single, in Sylvia's view very likely a closet homosexual.

Fortunately Sylvia was able to rely on Victor's gregarious nature to carry her family across the line on her wedding day. Eileen was reserved and distant, but in any case she went more or less unnoticed during the proceedings which were dominated by Michael's circle of admirers.

Michael's parents were long gone, thankfully. In-laws were not part of the plan Sylvia had for their life together, neither his nor hers. The only exception was her father, and she and Victor had established their own regular catch-ups long ago, ignoring the stilted relationships among the rest of her family.

It was still painful to watch her mother and father together at social occasions. They had not mellowed together now that they were old, and their lack of rapport was obvious, even to strangers. Luckily this was unremarkable in ageing married couples, most of whom, in Sylvia's experience, were more or less resigned to drifting along on a windless ocean, marooned with a person they no longer cared for, if they ever did.

Happily the mere fact that her parents were polite to each other, in spite of the undertow of disregard, still carried them through most social occasions, even the wedding of their eldest child.

In the end Michael decided that they had a great wedding day, replete with goodwill and harmony, and Sylvia was thankful for his rose-tinted take on the dislocated inner workings of her family, no doubt the product of Michael being a much-loved only child.

Despite her strong sense of independence and her cynicism about the institution of marriage, Sylvia did not hesitate to assume Michael's surname. She was now Sylvia Fontaine, and "Sylvia Rojo" was a thing of the past.

***

With Anna Kalajian's help, the removal of all traces of Isobel from GoodLord documents and images had been completed in advance of the wedding, allowing for a simple process of inserting Sylvia into the media spaces formerly occupied by Isobel. Except that this time around a lot of thought was given to making sure that the publicity shots reflected the right image for a new power couple on the social scene, with one eye on the world of politics.

Not long after the wedding prominent friends of the couple found themselves answering questions from reporters about Michael Fontaine's political ambitions, given his tremendous level of public support, and the need for decent people to enter politics. The declining standards in representation at both federal and state level across the country were a matter for concern.

"Australia is ready for someone like Michael Fontaine to stand for parliament and set an example to our politicians," Zelda Freestone said on TV. As Australia's richest mining magnate, she had the ear of anyone who mattered. A lot of folk at the big end of town agreed with her.

***

It was critical, of course, for the newly married couple to buy a new house together. They chose a large tasteful mansion in Brighton, a suburb still close to the bay, but with more social standing than the less desirable areas further down Beach Road.

Brighton was not far from Sylvia's parents, allowing her to drop in on her father when Eileen was out shopping. There was little she had to say to her mother, a lifetime of silent disapproval made it pointless, but Victor was a large part of any positive memories she had of childhood.

Their new home was also close to a golf course for Michael to indulge his obsession with a game that seemed to be focused mainly on socializing in the club bar.

It was painted white, and had two storeys, several bedrooms and bathrooms, and enough space downstairs for entertaining large gatherings of their closest friends and supporters.

There was a circular driveway in the huge front yard, covered in white gravel to match the house. The property was protected by a high fence and large steel gates, painted black. The gates were remotely controlled, designed to keep out well wishers and security risks alike. Huge double front doors, also black, were approached up a dozen steps, and the entrance-way was fitted with tall white columns.

The drought had reached the point where the shortage of water supplies was critical, with strict limits on water usage in the home and in gardens. They employed a landscape architect to install a drought-resistant garden, then hired a gardener to maintain it. So many trees and lawns were dying in the heat, it seemed to Sylvia that they would soon be growing cactus plants and not much else. Nonetheless, they planted some hardy native species, and the overall effect was impressive.

Before long, huge bushfires in eastern Victoria were causing black smoke to drift across Melbourne. Michael and Sylvia watched the news on TV, filled with reports of the bushfires, mostly human interest stories focused on the pain and suffering of people who lost their houses and loved ones to the fires, sobbing on camera as the news reporters pressed them for the grisly details of their traumatic experiences.

Half the state was ablaze, apparently, with massive damage and loss of life. Smoke and ash blew across Melbourne, to the amazement of the city's population, even though dangerous bushfires had occurred at regular intervals every few years or so ever since colonial times.

"God, it's terrible," Michael said, and immediately set about preparing a video message directly addressed to the victims of the bushfires, followed up with a Gathering offering up prayers for rain to end the drought.

Sylvia rarely visited the countryside. All she usually saw through the car windscreen when she did was endless kilometres of dry grass and empty paddocks, and she had no personal knowledge of most of the areas they mentioned in the news. Still, it was graphic and disturbing, and it seemed appropriate for GoodLord to start an appeal for donations for the victims of the fires. No one else in the country seemed to know what to do.

***

After a particularly exhausting day at work, Victor rang and told Sylvia that Eileen had been taken to hospital suffering from exhaustion.

"I'm seeing her tomorrow if you'd like to come to the hospital with me. She's expecting us around one pm, if that suits?"

Sylvia agreed, and arranged to pick Victor up at home, knowing that driving in the city was difficult for him these days.

When she arrived at the hospital with him, they found Eileen ensconced in a VIP suite on the ninth floor.

"Hello, dear," Eileen said weakly, glancing up at them. Sylvia wasn't sure who she was speaking to, but planted a dutiful kiss on her cheek and pulled up a chair, while Victor deposited some flowers on the bedside table.

It was a private hospital in East Melbourne, with all the comforts of a five star hotel, and the best doctors in town at your beck and call.

"They charge like a five star hotel, too," Victor had said during the drive into town. "But it's better to have the very best care, given that they're not too sure what's wrong."

However, Eileen looked her usual truculent self, with nothing in her manner that indicated ill health. Her florid face looked a little puffy, but her grey hair had recently been done with light blonde highlights, incongruous at her age. At least she still cared about these things.

"You're late, Victor," Eileen said.

"We agreed on one o'clock, my dear," Victor said mildly.

"Hmm," Eileen said, compressing her lips, as though Victor had confessed to an error.

"How are you, Mother?" Sylvia asked.

"I've been better," Eileen said. "These doctors don't seem to know what's wrong."

She sat up in bed and pointed to a vase full of flowers.

"Reverend Gordon was in to see me. He brought those. A real gentleman."

Sylvia remembered the vicar of Eileen's local church, a slight ingratiating man, apparently recently promoted to Canon in the Church, to Eileen's delight.

Eileen had ignored Victor's flowers, Sylvia noticed, as she launched into a list of her visitors, adding, "And Jack has been in twice this week. He said he was coming again today. He should be here soon."

Since this was Sylvia's first visit, the implications were clear. It was exhausting even just thinking about Eileen's endless complaints, direct or implied, and Sylvia simply murmured, "That's nice," and said little else, while wondering how she could leave before Jack arrived. Victor would probably want to stay, and she could hardly bundle him out early to avoid Jack.

Mercifully a nurse's aide came in at that point to check that everything was all right, and Sylvia got up from her chair and went to inspect the view from the window.

There was a view of a park across the road, carefully tended lawns and copses of deciduous trees in the European manner. Sylvia wondered idly if Eileen had anything wrong with her at all, or whether the administrative staff were indulging her hypochondria as the bills mounted up.

The aide offered them coffee, and Sylvia agreed, if only to fill in the visiting hour. She knew that Victor would stay longer than she could bear, and decided that she would follow up the coffee with a prolonged visit to the toilet.

However Jack arrived a moment later before Sylvia finished her coffee, calling out "Hello, everyone," as he entered, and without waiting for a response bowled over to Eileen's bedside and hugged her gently, planting a kiss on either cheek. The usual gushing routine of Eileen welcoming Jack with hugs and kisses erupted, Sylvia silently watching a display of affection worthy of a separation of several months.

"Mother! Looking lovely today! And as well as ever. You'll be out of here and back home in no time, mark my words."

Although Jack was nearly a decade younger than Sylvia, he had an oddly formal way of talking, which matched his three-piece suit, crisp white shirt, and a wavy blonde hairdo that almost matched Eileen's. Like Naomi he had inherited her short, plump, blonde looks, an offset to Victor and Sylvia, both of them tall and dark-skinned, with black curly hair, and an odd contrast when they were all together in one room.

All we need now is Naomi arriving to complete this little circus, Sylvia thought grimly, glancing at the clock on the wall and willing the visiting hour to hurry to a close.

It was a rare event for Sylvia and Jack to be in the same room at the same time. Sylvia usually saw Jack only at Christmas and birthdays, and the occasional wedding or funeral. In recent years, she had managed to be "out of town" for family birthdays, except Victor's, and Christmas was usually a flurry of hellos and goodbyes.

"How are you, son?" Victor said cheerily, and received the usual polite but distant reply. Despite Victor's love for Jack, there was little sign of it being reciprocated. Jack was on Eileen's side in their parents' endless uneasy truce.

Victor was very quiet on the drive home, and Sylvia assumed he was worried about Eileen's diagnosis. She didn't know what to say about it, so she spoke of other things, hoping to distract him.

A few days later Eileen was sent home, still without a definite diagnosis, but with instructions to get plenty of rest, and not exert herself.

"It was a very expensive 'we don't know' from the doctors," Victor said, "but at least your mother seems to have recovered a little."

Sylvia was certain that Eileen would outlast her father, and felt more concerned about him than her. She would be sure to be demanding all sorts of attention, sick or not.

She had to admit that, much as she loved her father, she could do without visits to her parents if it meant witnessing the final stage of what had been a dismal marriage.

***

Two weeks later Naomi rang in a state of shock.

"Mother's dead, Sylvia," she cried into the phone. Despite now being the mother of three kids to her great lumbering fool of a husband, Naomi still behaved like a wailing toddler when disaster struck. In this case she seemed to give no thought to the recipient of the phone call having to wade through the personal misery she imposed on them from a distance. Why she was so upset was a mystery to Sylvia, given Eileen's brusque treatment of them during childhood, and ever since, come to that.

Sylvia tried to say something, but the caterwauling at the other end of the phone made it impossible. After a few moments Sylvia said goodbye and rang off, deciding to ring her father for more details, and to make sure he was all right.

Victor was very quiet and contained, explaining that Eileen felt very ill and had been rushed to hospital, but it was too late to save her from the stroke that killed her a few hours later.

"I expected that she would have to go back into hospital, you know," Victor said sadly. "And then we could all have had time to go and see her when the end was near. But she declined so fast yesterday, and suddenly she was gone."

Sylvia arranged to see Victor the next day, feeling sad for him, but relieved that he was finally a free man. It would feel strange going to see him without Eileen in the background, nursing her resentments in another room, not wanting to talk, while simultaneously feeling ignored.

It was no surprise to Sylvia that a full scale church funeral was planned for Eileen, "a farewell to the community she loved so much," as the funeral brochure described it, in Jack's usual pompous style. For some reason he had taken over the running of the funeral.

Would you call it a "brochure," she wondered, sitting next to Victor in the family pew at St Stephen's, listening to the vicar wittering on about Eileen's wonderful contribution to the parish.

Victor stayed in the background, while Jack acted the role of the grieving favourite child to perfection, bravely keeping back the tears and delivering a funeral oration that rang with every variety of pious self regard. He referred incessantly to "our dear mother," a tear or two rolling down his pudgy little face, transforming Eileen from an embittered old woman into a latter day Christian matriarch, giver of life, a pillar of the community, a doting mother and a loving wife.

Sylvia squirmed in her pew, enduring what felt like half an hour of Jack's unctuous platitudes about the embittered woman who had destroyed her childhood, as well as the happiness of her father and the family in general, feeling a loathing for Jack that exceeded anything she had ever felt about him, despite the fact she had held him in contempt from the time he was a young child playing his mother off against the rest of them.

She held her tongue, concealing her rage with a poker face, so that when Michael murmured beside her that Jack "obviously loved your mother very much," he said nothing when she didn't answer, probably assuming she was overwhelmed with grief.

Sylvia was keenly aware of the fact that people were paying close attention to Michael and her from the surrounding pews, Michael's fame preceding him and bringing a larger crowd and more attention than even Jack could reasonably have hoped for.

Mercifully no one else spoke, and moments after the service ended Sylvia was able to plead work commitments and escape in the limo with Michael before she lost her temper and told Jack what she thought of him.

In the long run, so far as she was concerned, Eileen's death was a pitiful end to a meaningless life.

***

Unbeknown to Michael Fontaine, Sylvia was in constant consultation with Freddie Wu.

"The Federal scene is best for Michael," Freddie said to Sylvia as they sat up in bed one afternoon in a penthouse with a view of the bay. "The thing is, we need a national crisis that will create a public outcry for him to lead the way."

"What sort of crisis?" Sylvia asked.

"It doesn't matter much, so long as it is a national crisis. Something economic, perhaps. A share market collapse. Of course, let's not forget terrorism. National security is always a sure fire bet to get voters worried. Or a disaster like bushfires. Similar to the recent Victorian ones, only on a national scale."

"There'll be plenty of opportunities with bushfires. They happen every summer, and they seem to be getting bigger every year. Especially with this never-ending drought."

"Yes, you might be right. It's simply a matter of waiting for the right moment."

However, first things first. There was still a lot to be done in grooming Fontaine for a political career. He was being courted by both major political parties, showered with invitations that

Anna Kalajian sifted through looking for the best opportunities. However, the specifics of his entry to politics were still unclear.

Public profile was no problem for Fontaine. The challenge was to achieve some level of political autonomy in whatever direction he took. He viewed both political parties with dismay, like a handsome but poverty-stricken young man looking for an attractive young heiress, but finding no one who appealed to him in the least.

"Both parties are just a gang of crooks, so far as I'm concerned," he said to Sylvia and Freddie one day. "I'm a realist. I know that power requires ruthless decisions at times, for the common good. But surely God would prefer a ruthless politician who gives a damn about the people he represents. It doesn't seem too much to ask, does it?"

Freddie smiled. "You are quite right, Michael. And not only are they crooked, both parties are filled with mediocre time-servers. It seems almost a given in modern politics, I'm afraid."

"I don't want my ministry in this life to be downgraded to some sort of mud wrestling for power. I would rather go it alone."

"Good idea," Freddie said. "In any case, there's no way you would be granted leadership of one of the major parties. Or even, perhaps, a prominent position. They are both simply looking for more votes for a win in a marginal seat. I suggest that you stand for the Senate, as your own man. Then you could win power and influence to a large degree on your own, but with our help, of course."

"That's a wonderful idea, isn't it Michael?" Sylvia said. "Senators can be quite powerful, can't they, Freddie?"

"Yes, indeed. Look at Senator Brian Harradine from Tasmania. A one-man political party. Tremendously influential for decades."

"That sounds like it might be a good way to go," Fontaine said cautiously.

"Yes," said Freddie. "You won't need to belong to a political party. Just simply stand for the Senate as an independent."

"We should examine the possibilities," Sylvia said to Michael. "You'll have all the help you need."

"And the votes of millions of supporters who love your TV shows, even if they are not all members of GoodLord," said Freddie.

"Yes, I see what you mean," Fontaine said. "My policies would be my own. No kowtowing to big business and the trade unions."

"Well put, Michael," said Freddie.

Sylvia knew that Michael Fontaine saw himself as a man of the people, son of an undertaker, someone who pulled himself up by his bootstraps in service to the Lord.

"It sounds ideal, darling," she said to Fontaine, smiling into his face.

Freddie nodded, and clapped him on the back. "The time is right, Michael," he said.

***

The immediate issue before Sylvia was how to get to first base, given that the Senate election outcome was unpredictable. Any outcome that relied on a vote was never a sure thing, as even the most seasoned politicians learned to their cost. That was democracy for you.

As always, Freddie Wu was the best sounding board, a man who could respond succinctly to any scenario that came up. His instincts were very similar to Sylvia's, but of course he had decades of experience in the cut-throat world of Shanghai politics, whereas she was still on a steep learning curve. Not that he talked about his early days much, apart from the occasional funny story about rival politicians fighting to the death over the spoils extorted from a hapless population.

Still, as Freddie always said to her, having the right instincts for political struggle was more than half the battle.

The icing on the cake was that GoodLord members had a built-in belief system that exceeded the devotion of clients and customers of any brand in existence, even sporting clubs, movie star fans and fashion houses.

Since the GoodLord congregation was slavishly devoted to Michael, the donations kept rolling in, meaning that revenues were very strong indeed. And Charlotte Hung had developed a ruthlessly efficient finance department which was growing exponentially to keep pace with GoodLord's explosive national expansion.

Charlotte was quietly efficient, and minded her own business, making no attempt in her dealings with Sylvia to exploit her own relationship with Freddie Wu. Sylvia appreciated her discretion, having initially wondered whether Charlotte would try to manipulate her relationship with Freddie to her own advantage. This increased her level of trust in Charlotte, insofar as anyone could be trusted.

***

The election campaign spilt over into their home, with increased security and more cars needed for all the comings and goings of campaign staff to meetings and events in the early morning and late evening. Sylvia's already busy life became a maelstrom of messages by mobile phone, landline, email, and letter, as well as personal visits by well wishers, glad handers, and all sorts of people offering donations, many of them making demands in exchange.

Anna Kalajian became absorbed in arranging short videos for the internet, showing Michael at his best mingling with the people, spreading goodwill and a feeling of belonging to a public stressed by drought and financial crises. Michael was very adept at these performances, and Anna was able to arrange dozens of brief clips of his cheerful interactions with folk from all walks of life, produced to a professional standard by the GoodLord media company.

Michael's level of celebrity increased tenfold. Now, with his face in the national media as a potential senator with an evangelical following, every appearance in public became a cavalcade of loud attention.

Sylvia took to travelling incognito, wearing sunglasses and a hat, and leaving her BMW in the garage in favour of a dull grey Honda.

Michael, on the other hand, lapped up the attention, and upgraded to a large Mercedes-Benz, complete with Alex, the driver for their Mornington lost weekend, as a uniformed chauffeur cum bodyguard. Michael would also invariably be attended on by a couple of GoodLord Inc staff, including Anna Kalajian, as her role as Michael's minder on public occasions expanded.

Anna was adept at directing Michael through crowds, managing the press, and attracting just the right amount of attention to their entourage whenever it was needed in childcare centres, nursing homes, factories and all the rest of the stopovers required of aspiring politicians who want to curry favour with the public. The appearances were designed for maximum media attention, making it easier to keep Michael motivated. And of course, Michael was far more likely to follow the "suggestions" of an attractive young woman like Anna than any male member of staff, or any woman he wasn't attracted to.

In some ways, Anna was standing in for Sylvia, who limited her own public appearances to the more glamorous events, such as a night at the opera, or a charity event that attracted the big names of Melbourne's social scene, from celebrity hairdressers to famous cricketers.

Sylvia would also drag Michael along to smaller, more select gatherings with the real powerbrokers, from the old money descendants of Victoria's Western District graziers, to news media barons, property developers, and business leaders from the big end of town. These were the people that Freddie Wu cultivated, at the sort of events that Freddie was prone to attend as he relentlessly networked his way around the A-list.

While Michael would complain about "hobnobbing with the nobs," it was obvious to Sylvia that despite himself he loved all the attention from important people, giving the stamp of approval for his dreams of success.

***

With the election looming, Sylvia instructed Anna Kalajian to match the upcoming MCG bookings against the election dates. Three major Gatherings were staged in the run-up to the election, and televised nationally.

Sylvia limited herself to brief appearances onstage, appearing in the VIP seats just to one side of the speaker's rostrum, and joining Michael at the microphone to pump their joined hands in the air as he introduced her to a roar from the crowd of a hundred thousand fans. Then she would discreetly slip offstage when the first musical item was scheduled, take a secure elevator to the underground car park, and go to her office to catch up on her busy schedule.

She didn't pore over the polling results with Michael and Freddie. Her focus was on checking Michael's general state of mind and propping him up whenever he slid into gloom.

For all his charisma and good cheer, Michael was prone to swift changes of mood, from elation to catastrophizing. This depressive streak was annoying, but thankfully usually brief. At these times, he talked of tossing in his political ambitions, and returning to his ministry, rekindling the good old days.

To add to the stress, as the election came closer Michael's polling numbers were still looking good, but so were the numbers for Sam Newbold.

One evening at home as they sat in the lounge having an after dinner drink Michael said that he was feeling dubious about his prospects of winning the election.

"The Lord will provide, my love," Sylvia said.

"Don't take the piss," Michael said mildly. One of the things that Sylvia liked about him was that he didn't let his calling get in the way of his blunt language, at least in private. He also enjoyed a drink, especially whisky.

Sylvia laughed, and poured him another glass.

"Freddie says the odds for a win are good."

"I would prefer the odds to be bloody stupendously in my favour. You know what these polls are like."

"Let's forget about that now, Michael. Time to relax."

"Yes, you're right," he said. "Let's watch the footy."

They turned on the TV, and as it happened, Richmond football club won their fifth straight game of the season, leaving Michael flushed and cheerful as they worked their way through the whisky bottle.

By the time they tumbled into bed he was king of all he surveyed, a man on the way to the Senate, by God.

CHAPTER 8

HARRY

Over the years I've done my best to forget Neil Bautervich, journalist-cum-spymaster, the unpleasant little arsehole who informed me back in the day of anti Vietnam War protests that I had to rat on the radical Maoist students or lose my university scholarship.

But there he is in Poynton's Pub, decades later, although by now the old student dive is gone, and a refurbished version has taken its place. It looks as though it aspires to be a wine bar, but someone has forgotten to tell the locals. It's still filled with hordes of drunken students, middle aged male office workers leering at young females, and a vibrant cross-section of the pretentious hangers-on that swarm like flies around university pubs.

This time I approach Neil at his table, rather than sitting and waiting for him to come and spoil my day.

"Neil!" I say. "Long time no see. Harry Mott. I used to be a spotty youth with a beard and long hair, ringing you up every Monday at lunchtime with hot tips from the student barricades."

He looks up at me, and then at his drinking companion, a fat doleful man in an ill-fitting suit, pasty faced and looking bored to death. After a few moments I realize that Neil's mate is utterly drunk, but that probably makes little difference to his dopy appearance. I'm hoping I've interrupted some confidential exchange of state secrets, but that obviously isn't the case.

"Well, yes. How are you, Harry?" Neil is all smiles, winking at his tubby mate. "Those were the days, were they not?"

"Yes indeed," I say.

I have an odd feeling that this is no accident, but maybe I'm overreacting.

"This is my comrade-in-arms, Hugh," says Neil.

Tubs, as I immediately think of him, struggles to his feet and sticks out a plump white hand.

"Pleasedtomeetyou," he mumbles. He does smile, however, a ghastly leer that looks like he's about to throw up.

"Same here," I say to him.

"Hugh has a couple of tips for me," says Neil. "Racing tips, that is."

"Didn't know you were a gambler, Neil."

"Just occasionally."

He smiles too, a little more convincingly than his mate Hugh. Neil's gained a little weight and his hair has gone a distinguished grey, but he still has that glint in his eye, the professional nosey parker who missed out on a glamorous career as a TV quiz show host and has poured his energy into various displacement activities to make up for it.

"Still a journalist in the shittiest tabloid in town, are we, Neil?" I say, in the nastiest manner I can muster.

"Editor, now Harry, for my sins. But look, Hugh and I have to get back to the office. I'll give you my mobile number. I have some information that could be very important to you."

"To me? Last time around, that didn't work out too well."

"That was different," he says, and I'll be fucked if I can't detect a hint of apology in his voice. How can that be, from such a slithering little snake like him?

He hands me his card, pats Tubs on the shoulder, they drain their beers, and off they go, the Laurel and Hardy of whatever shit show they work for.

***

We are back in Poynton's Pub by the end of the week, staring at each other across a table loaded with unrecovered used glasses and puddles of spilt beer.

"Well, what do you want?" I ask. "An update on Sam Newbold's doings? Or Melissa Frankel? I can't help you. I have other things to do with my life."

Neil looks at me tolerantly.

"I can understand your resentment, Harry," he says. "But this is a two-way street. Like I said, I have information that will be useful to you."

"What do you want in return?"

"We need your input on some recent developments in the political field."

"Christ!" I say, feeling rage overtaking me. I have to grip the edge of the table to stop myself throwing my beer in Neil's face.

"Take it easy. Like I said, a two-way street. We will keep you informed of the activities of your opponents. And your allies."

I swallow hard, and say something like fuck off you little prick, but Neil just smiles, waiting patiently.

"Come on, Harry," he says after another sip of beer. "You know that we can still destroy your career. You're the police spy in that little bit of ancient history during the Vietnam War. Not Sam Newbold. That would come as a shock to Noah Kowalski and the gang, don't you think? All those loved-up lefties trying to climb the greasy pole to fame and fortune. Nothing much has changed."

"Fuck you," I mutter.

"Let's face it," Neil says. "Youthful indiscretions generally have a way of coming back to bite you. But the good news this time around is that your assistance will bring with it an increase in your earnings."

"Assistance doing what?"

"Well, things are changing in the area of political donations, as I'm sure you're aware."

"Can you be more specific?"

"Donations to Australian political parties from mainland Chinese living in Australia are now a matter of interest to us."

"Haven't seen much of that. Just the odd contribution."

"Well, we have reason to believe that it's all going to change very soon. And we want to get ahead of it."

"OK. What's involved?"

Neil looks around casually, as though expecting a waiter to deliver the duck à l'orange.

"I want you to accept money from Chinese donors. Go along with what they suggest. And keep me informed about how it all works out."

"I don't know any Chinese donors."

"That's where I can help you," Neil says. "Charlotte Hung is a very influential member of the Chinese community. We have word from an MP's office in her electorate that she is interested in donating to politicians."

"One of your spies in a Labour MP's office?" I say.

"Who said it was a Labour MP? It's just a tip-off from someone in our network. We are interested in finding out more. You need to meet up with Charlotte for lunch. Put her name and number into your phone." And he gives me a scrap of paper.

I put the details into my phone, and hand back the slip of paper.

"OK," I say. "What do you want me to do once I've met Charlotte Hung?"

"Accept her offer, and introduce her to Noah Kowalski," Neil says. "Let me know how you go, what the money is used for. Presumably to boost Sam Newbold's chances in the Senate election campaign."

"What about Melissa Frankel? Are you still keeping tabs on her?"

"No, they tell me she's no longer directly involved in politics now, more interested in human rights."

"OK, what next?"

"Ring me Monday at midday. Just like old times."

"Fond memories," I say sourly. "Who's driving all this? Our US allies? The CIA, I suppose? Scared that China is going to eat their lunch?"

"Not at all. We're well ahead of the Yanks on this one."

Neil sits back in his chair, lifting his beer in salute as I stumble towards the door. I have that familiar sinking feeling again.

***

Noah Kowalski is more than pleased with the news about Charlotte Hung and her interest in donating to the Party.

"I called by her office and had a chat. She's offered me good money for an introduction to you," I tell him. "Plus a retainer if things work out."

"I hope that hasn't affected your judgement at all, mate?" he grins at me.

"Not in the least," I deadpan.

"Glad to hear it," he laughed. "How did you come across her?"

"An old mate from uni days referred her to me."

"Good one. This could be the shot in the arm we need. Just as we're looking down the barrel of more time in the wilderness! We'll need a landslide to win the next election, and that won't come cheap."

He stands up and looks out from his office window at the view of the State Houses of Parliament in the distance, a statue of some nineteenth century colonial grandee barely visible at the top of the one hundred or so steps to the massive columns at the entrance. Nothing like a statue of someone you never heard of in front of Parliament, with the obligatory pigeon shit on its head, to enhance your opinion of the heart of democracy in our fine state.

"We're looking at two things from them," I say. "Large cash donations to the Party. And huge property deals, construction work, and so on, that they want us to facilitate."

"Sounds good," says Noah. "We need to get them past talking and into getting results."

"First step is to meet them," I say. "Lunch next week, say Tuesday? They'd like to meet you as their guest at their favourite restaurant, the Golden Dragon."

"Yeah, I know it," Noah said. "OK, then, Tuesday. I want you there with me, of course, Harry. If this means large amounts of cash donations, and I certainly fucking hope it does, I'll need you to take care of that. I don't want anyone else involved."

"Yeah, sure," I say.

I don't mind being his courier. Messing about with huge amounts of cash can't be delegated to just anybody, and we need to put limits on who knows what. And it was my baby, thanks to Neil Bautervich.

Noah is pacing up and down, in a cheerful sort of way, rubbing his hands together like a cartoon character, say a bank robber about to open the vault.

"With a bit of luck," he says, "if we can put together a group of these people throwing their money at us, this will save our arses."

It'll save mine too. Nothing like a late career boost to give a silver lining to the looming prospect of retirement.

***

The lunch for Noah to meet Charlotte Hung goes like a dream. She introduces us to her husband, George Hung, a tall, fat jolly opportunist wearing a winter navy suit with white shirt and blue tie, despite the fact it's the middle of summer, and warm indoors as the aircon struggles with the heat. It's one of Melbourne's heatwave days, although searing dry heat around forty degrees Celsius is becoming more and more common during the endless drought.

Apparently Charlotte is a qualified accountant and financial expert with her own consultancy. She's nicely plump without being overweight like her husband. A pleasant round face, straight black hair in a fringe, glasses and a big smile enlarged by a heavy dash of rich red lipstick makes me feel welcome as we exchange pleasantries.

Noah is smiling and amiable, thanking Charlotte and George for the invitation to lunch. It's a side of him I don't see very often, and I put it down to the smell of money and the prospect of an expensive free meal.

After a minute or two we're joined by an older man called Freddie Wu, a smooth talking character, clearly the dominant figure in their group. Not that Freddie hogs the conversation. He shows a genial interest in everyone, while silently taking stock of Noah. It is clear, with no one actually saying so, that Freddie is the money man at the table.

We are in a private room, sitting around a circular dining table with heavy black chairs, red serviettes, colourful wall hangings with Chinese calligraphy, and an endless cycle of waiters scuttling in and out with new dishes, making for a bustling tableau even more challenging to the senses than my first experience of a formal dinner at a university shindig, when I was confronted by a table loaded with more crockery, cutlery and wine glasses than I had ever seen before in my life.

The waiters keep coming back and plonking more dishes on the table, and there's a clatter of Mandarin between Charlotte and George as each course arrives. The business of eating takes up most of our lunch time, course after course of delicacies appearing with magical regularity, all accompanied by Charlotte's explanations of what each dish is, and its significance for your health.

"Lotus root, good for your skin," she says cheerily to Noah and me, pointing at what looks like parsnip gone wrong languishing in a bowl of an unidentified fluid. It's the only dish I don't like the look of, and thankfully there are also various delicious meat dishes done a dozen different ways, and vegetables and rice ditto. Even more thankfully, there are no shellfish, which brings me out in a rash.

Freddie restricts himself to a few words of Mandarin with George, while Charlotte, Noah and I exchange pleasantries, me trying to get my chopstick skills back into gear to pinion the delicacies in front of me.

As lunch comes near to a close, Freddie Wu looks at Noah, and points out the window of the restaurant at the sign for a multi-storey car park on the other side of the Chinatown laneway, as if directing his attention to a local landmark.

"Noah, let's talk business. I always think the frank approach is best." Freddie says, "As proof of my good intentions, I have taken the liberty of bringing with me an immediate donation to your Party. It is sitting in the boot of my car in two large bags in that carpark. If you would be so kind as to call a car to take care of it, I can hand it to you now."

Noah smiles, and says, "Very thoughtful of you, Mr Wu."

"Call me Freddie," Wu says, and waves to a solid-looking Chinese guy who has just appeared at the door to our private room. How he knows when to appear, I don't know. Maybe the room is bugged. Could be that Freddie owns the restaurant and has it wired for sound. Who the hell knows.

Anyhow, I lean over to Noah and murmur, "my car is parked a few minutes away. I can go with Freddie's mate and fix it now."

Noah nods, and turns back to Freddie.

"No problem, Freddie. Harry here can take care of business right now, as you suggest."

Freddie smiles beatifically, the picture of the rich uncle bestowing a small fortune on a favourite nephew at his twenty-first birthday party.

"Wonderful, wonderful," Freddie says. "Very kind of you, Harry. My driver, Fong, will show you the way to my car."

I follow Fong to a Volvo parked in the multi-storey carpark across the road. He opens the boot and shows me two large zipped bags, much like the huge gym bags a young guy would lug to footy training.

Fong nods and smiles and hands me a plastic carpark card. Obviously to allow me re-entry when I come back in my car. I don't know if he speaks English, but he doesn't need to.

I walk quickly to my own carpark a couple of blocks away, leap into the Camry and do my best to cruise slowly back to Fong and the mystery bags. The thought of that much loot makes me want to plant my foot and screech down the narrow Chinatown laneways back to the Golden Dragon, maybe honking the horn and sideswiping parked cars and driving on the footpath, scattering pedestrians on all sides in my hurry to grab the bags and… do what with them? Noah and I haven't anticipated this move, not today. But, first get the bags, then work out what you do with a boot full of cash.

When I get back to Fong and Freddie's Volvo, Fong indicates that I park next to him. I guess they've reserved this extra parking space somehow specially for this moment. Maybe Freddie owns the carpark as well.

The transaction is over in seconds, Fong effortlessly tossing the bags in my boot as though they are empty. I wonder about leaving all this cash in my car boot, but then I notice a young Chinese man standing guard by the elevator, and realize that all is safe.

Then Fong refuses to take the plastic carpark card back from me, waving dismissively and leading me back to the Golden Dragon. All neatly planned.

When Noah and I leave Charlotte Hung and Freddie Wu after many toasts of mao-tai, I tell Noah what happened.

"Leave the bags in your boot for the moment," he says. "I'll ring the boys to collect the cash from you later on."

Ready cash is the lifeblood of politics, and no mistake. You can call it corruption if you like, but show me a political party that hasn't got its snout in the trough, and I'll show you a party that's on the skids. That's how the world works, whether you sign up with Al Capone or Mother Teresa.

***

"So what are all these doings with Charlotte Hung about?" I ask Neil in our next face-to-face meeting to report my success with Charlotte, yet again in Poynton's. No one takes any notice of drinking buddies, Neil once said, and Poynton's Pub is as good a place as any, with its diverse clientele and large crowds of drinkers spilling out onto the pavement on sunny days.

"The Chinese Government is encouraging its nationals, mostly businessmen, to infiltrate overseas politics with donations and other forms of influence," Neil says.

"How can the Chinese Government enforce a policy like that? Aren't Chinese businessmen out to make money for themselves, like any other businessmen?"

"They don't have to enforce it," he says. "All Chinese overseas are expected to do the bidding of the Chinese Government. Become a member of the Communist Party, expand your business and your personal and business networks, while at the same time pleasing the Party."

"But the Chinese have been doing business all over the world for ages. What's new about all this?"

"It's all a matter of scale," Neil says. "Point is, now we're looking at a full-scale offensive to obtain political influence, all paid for. And we need you to help us monitor it."

"But I'm not sure I can do it."

"We need your help," Neil repeats slowly.

"We?"

"It's a major national security issue. We need to track who is involved in all these foreign donations to political parties, what influence the money is buying, who people like Charlotte Hung work for. Fill in the blanks."

"What do you mean, people like Charlotte Hung?"

"Cashed-up mainland Chinese with connections to the Communist Party. In Charlotte's case, she gained permanent residence here after the Tiananmen Square riots in 1989."

"When Bob Hawke gave an amnesty to Chinese students staying in Australia?" I say.

"Yes. A huge security blunder for a Prime Minister to make," Neil said. "Some of those students were bona fide refugees. Most of them were not. A significant minority were Communist Party members reporting back to Beijing."

"So what's Charlotte Hung's story?"

"We think she has an uncle who is a Communist Party boss in Nanjing."

So now Neil has added an appeal to patriotism to my first briefing from him after all these years. A stellar day in our ongoing relationship.

This latest twist in events has me worried. I can't tell Ben Reilly about these donations coming through Charlotte Hung, especially as Noah Kowalski is now fully committed to the whole deal. Ben is just too honest, there's no way he'd accept it, and there's no way the deal can be cancelled.

Nor can I tell anyone else. Certainly not Rita, who has a very strict moral code against all forms of dealings in what you might call the grey areas of business and politics.

***

A whole new world opens up as our Chinese donors grow from a steady stream to a raging torrent. Much of my work becomes focused on the logistics and security of managing large amounts of cash. It's like all my Christmases are coming at once.

When I tell Charlotte Hung at one of our meetings over lunch that I am taking some leave for a holiday, she invites me to visit China.

"Your wife must come too. We would be very happy to have you as our guests, it will be a pleasure," Charlotte says.

"Really? That would be great!" I say, and I mean it. Noah must have had a word to Charlotte. He's been with them to China several times, coming back saying how impressive it is, and how I should take a trip there.

Since our honeymoon in Europe in 1980, Rita and I have only travelled overseas together a couple of times, to Bali and Thailand. This is mainly because I hate being a tourist, so I feel a bit guilty about not taking her on a decent overseas holiday.

Ten days later we land in Beijing, our first stopover, and book into a plush hotel as the guests of Charlotte and George Hung.

The hotel foyer is all marble and chandeliers, about the size of the inside of a large warehouse, and who knows how many storeys high. We're booked into an executive suite, complete with fawning staff constantly knocking on the door to give us something complementary, or deliver room service, my personal idea of paradise. I'm glad we're not paying for it, since even a cup of coffee costs ten dollars, and I don't bother checking the price of anything else.

It's autumn, the mild weather giving us a break from the early summer heat already arriving in Melbourne's spring, and perfect for me to give tourism a chance. Charlotte and George take us to see the sights, Tiananmen Square, the Forbidden City. Everything seems large, exotic, the sort of stuff you involuntarily point at and tell your companions to look at. Even the names are entrancing.

Then we end up with a fabulous dinner in an expensive restaurant, and have a late night eating and drinking far too much, and watching singers in traditional dress performing excerpts from Chinese opera, a form of entertainment which must have been devised for the purpose of torturing foreign tourists.

The next day we visit the Ming tombs. Charlotte and George send us off with a guide, a young woman who is either an employee or a relative, I'm not sure which. A student, they tell us, smiling and shy, who reels off the details of the famous emperors buried in this massive cemetery.

It's as though she's swallowed a tourist brochure whole. Or maybe some chapters from an encyclopedia. Perfect English sentences tumble out of her mouth, full of unlikely terms and academic language, 'this most famous of China's emperors', and so on. Is it possible to memorize such a huge chunk of text and deliver it verbatim? Someone once told me about a Chinese university student they knew who carried around a Pocket Oxford Dictionary of English, committing a page to memory each day. Maybe it is possible, after all.

I'm so struck with this girl's feat of memory I totally ignore the content, not that I care that much, to be honest. I would much rather read about it, and I'd remember more that way too. Still, she's glowing with pride in her country, and it's worth watching her perform her party trick, so that we force a huge tip on her afterwards.

She seems grateful. Is it possible to be a penniless student if you are related to Charlotte Hung? I doubt it, so I guess she is no poor cousin. Maybe the daughter of their housekeeper, or whatever.

On we go to more sightseeing. Then it's back on the plane again, to Tianjin, Wuhan, and Hangzhou, flying in business class. Huge cities come and go, even bigger lunches and dinners. Rita and I sometimes fly alone together, at other times with Charlotte and George, or some relative, friend or employee of theirs.

Where do they get all this energy, we wonder? Everywhere they go they're greeted like royalty. How could two youngish people have this kind of clout? Their guanxi would need massive scales manufactured to weigh trucks to calculate the heft of it all.

As we travel on, city to city, taking photos on our phones of almost everything we see, Charlotte and George are in their element, bursting with pride in their homeland, from the history of its ancient civilization to its rebirth as a modern superpower.

The sheer size and magnificence of absolutely everything. Gigantic modern cities, all of them it seems with a population of at least ten million people. Lavish restaurants, ancient monuments. Abundant poverty too, just to add colour for the average tourist. An old man struggling uphill on a push bike with a mattress tied to his back. Migrant workers, meaning labourers from other provinces, living 24/7 in half-built apartment blocks, visible from our hotel moving about with lamps after dark. But there's no doubt about the rise of China's middle class, with modern buildings, a gazillion cars, and shopping to die for.

Everything is on such a large scale, it makes a city like Melbourne, with a few million people, feel like a country town.

Rita, like me, loves it all, but by our second-last day we are exhausted by the endless round of lunches and dinners and sightseeing. However, we manage to score a day off from our official duties, which is what it feels like, and spend the next day in bed at the hotel, watching movies in our room.

I ring Billie on my mobile, and she marvels at receiving a call from China. She's in her eighties now, and is impressed that mobile phones mean instant communication from anywhere.

"Hi, Billie," I say, "I'm in China!" in case she's forgotten. But she still has all her marbles, and she's still full of beans.

"You're such a long way away," she says, "but you sound like you're in the same room." I've been trying to talk her into moving into a retirement home, worried about her living alone, but she refuses point blank. "I've got nice neighbours, Harry," she says. "I'm better off staying put." I hope I have her resilience at her age, supposing I make it that far.

At the moment I'm so knackered I can hardly talk, and after a few more exchanges we ring off, and I wonder again about how happy Billie is, in the final stages of such a hard life.

"I feel like I'm wagging it from school," Rita says as I stretch out on the bed again, "or taking a sickie when I'm not really sick."

I know what she means. It's a welcome break from a demanding schedule, and it's hard to keep up.

***

Dinner that night turns out to be yet another superb restaurant, although when we are in the limo that Charlotte sent for us I notice alleyways nearby with skinny grubby kids playing in the dirt, and wonder what they've eaten today. Wealth is cheek by jowl with poverty here, much less kept at arm's length like it is at home.

We are welcomed at the door by restaurant staff guiding us every step of the way to our private dining room, or Charlotte's, anyway. And there she is with George, both smiling a great big welcome, the happiest husband and wife in all of China.

There's the usual gaggle of people we won't be talking to, even though we are introduced with much smiling and laughing, presumably because they don't speak English and we don't speak Mandarin. They seem to play the role of extras at these dinners, or maybe they are relatives and friends who are owed a meal for some reason.

"We love Australia," Charlotte beams at us, and proposes a toast, and George smiles and nods his head.

Of course Rita and I return the toast, with compliments about China, a wonderful country, and thank you for such an exciting trip.

We return to gabbing about the food served up to us, and the tourist attractions we've seen. Rita is still doing an excellent job of keeping up the pleasant chit-chat, but as time passes I feel myself sinking into the sort of personal fog that formal occasions always bring on. It's too much like being in some outlandish play where I keep forgetting the script.

It's bad enough on my home ground. I'm hopeless at paying attention during ceremonies and formal dinners, and usually drift off as I drink too much and long for a cigarette. At least here on this occasion I can smoke my head off, as the males at the table cheerfully fill the ashtrays placed near them.

"China is a world of its own," Rita says when we return to our hotel, and I can only agree, feeling overwhelmed by my impressions of a culture that seems so much larger than life.

At this point it dawns on me what a juggernaut China is. Australia's population is simply a flyspeck by comparison. It will take a lot of nuclear missiles to repel China in the Pacific, if things turn nasty, that's certain.

On the other hand, it is on this trip that I first encounter Hainanese chicken rice, a meal to die for. Why would the country that invented Hainanese chicken rice want to invade Australia? I ask myself. They have everything they could possibly need on their own doorstep.

PART THREE

WELCOME ABOARD

CHAPTER 9

SYLVIA

The text message from Freddie Wu arrived during a meeting at the city offices of GoodLord Inc. Sylvia glanced at her mobile screen, and closed the meeting. "Fong will pick you up at 2.15 pm usual place," the message read.

She walked a couple of blocks to an underground car park in Chinatown, and found Fong parked near the elevator in Freddie's Volvo. She greeted him and sat in the back seat busy with her iPad until they reached Freddie's building and parked underneath it. Moments later they were together in yet another anonymous penthouse.

"A good trip to Jakarta?" she asked Freddie.

He smiled and poured her a drink at the cadenza.

"Yes," he said. "Although Jakarta is a very complex place, and there wasn't much time to do any long term planning."

They stood together, relaxed with their drinks, looking at the view across the docks to the Westgate Bridge.

"However, I had time on the flight back to do some thinking about the election campaign," Freddie went on. "For example, at this point in the Senate election race, we need to own a high level member of the Labour Party to help you beat Sam Newbold."

"Who do you have in mind?"

"There is a fellow called Noah Kowalski, working here in Melbourne. He might just be the person we need," Freddie said, pursing his lips.

"Don't know him."

"Yes, he is not a public figure. He is what they call a numbers man. Very powerful."

"Can I help you?" Sylvia asked.

"I think perhaps you can. Noah Kowalski is successful at what he does, but frustrated. We need to improve his present life, and offer him a better future."

"It could be hard to shift a committed Labour man."

"Yes. However, I hear that he has a substantial gambling problem, and therefore a shortage of funds. Plus Labour has no prospect of being in power for a very long time. Perhaps you can assist in drawing him in to support Michael."

"Yes, of course. How do I get to meet him?"

"Charlotte Hung has contacts amongst his colleagues. We can use Charlotte as a go-between."

"OK. Sounds interesting."

"Yes. Noah Kowalski is an interesting man."

It was unusual for Freddie to make this sort of comment, and Sylvia wondered what the best approach to Noah Kowalski might be. But of course, Freddie would provide an impeccable briefing, and somehow devise the perfect plan.

Obviously Charlotte Hung had already been involved in this initial approach to Noah Kowalski, and Freddie had not told Sylvia. But then again, she didn't tell Freddie everything herself, and realistically their different agendas would never be a perfect match. And Charlotte was very talented.

At first Sylvia had found Charlotte's unfailing charm and cheerfulness faintly annoying. Why weren't there a few knots in the grain? That constant calm and politeness felt artificial, a Girl Guide's attempt to win more brownie points.

Gradually, though, Sylvia began to understand the street fighter behind the mask of diplomacy. Outside the GoodLord inner circle, in dealings with contractors and business associates, Charlotte could force the opposition to surrender in a blink, a suave caring dentist suddenly yanking out a tooth with a pair of rusty pliers.

Observing Charlotte at times like this was a real pleasure, and Sylvia came to view her artistry with a mix of admiration and unease. Clearly she was skilled and ambitious, and potentially a threat if she became a competitor. On the other hand, Freddie Wu ran a tight ship, and there was no doubt that Charlotte Hung was on the fast track to big things, with or without GoodLord.

***

It wasn't long before Sylvia was introduced to Noah Kowalski at a dinner hosted by Charlotte, with George Hung, Charlotte's husband, and Freddie Wu in attendance.

The dinner was a small private function in a Chinese restaurant, with Noah Kowalski arriving alone, no doubt as requested. Sylvia and Noah were the only non-Chinese in the room, and Freddie introduced her as the CEO of GoodLord and the wife of Michael Fontaine.

"Sylvia was a successful business executive before she joined GoodLord and married Michael," Freddie added.

Noah was an ugly little man, with a larrikin manner. Not that he was rude or disrespectful. On the contrary, he had a rough charm that his Chinese audience seemed to like, laughing and talking with him from the beginning of the meal. He obviously was already at ease in the lead up to this important next step in the relationship.

Sylvia knew little of China and its customs. However, she had learned a great deal from Freddie Wu, and she could see clearly how easy it would be for an Australian politician like Noah Kowalski to underestimate Freddie and Charlotte.

They were certainly prepared to spend big to entertain prospective business partners at formal business lunches. On the other hand, they were effusive and friendly beyond the usual Australian business norms, and clearly expected a level of reciprocity unfamiliar to Westerners. Despite the excellent English of both Freddie and Charlotte, Sylvia still wondered what they made of Noah's sardonic sense of humour, and his failure to compliment his hosts at every opportunity.

Nonetheless, they laughed at his stories about Australian Prime Ministers. How one had disappeared while snorkelling in the sea off Portsea, rumoured to have been kidnapped by a Chinese submarine. How another had died "on the job," a phrase that Freddie had to translate for Charlotte, much to her amusement. And yet another Australian Prime Minister had turned up at his hotel reception desk in the USA early one morning totally befuddled and minus his trousers. All true stories, Noah insisted, which Sylvia knew to be a fact. How could you make up stories as absurd as these? And all of them were conservative Coalition prime ministers, of course.

Towards the end of the meal Freddie turned to Noah and said: "I gather that you haven't met Sylvia before?"

"That's right," Noah said. "An unexpected pleasure!" he added gallantly. "I've seen you on TV, though. Your wedding day," he said to Sylvia.

"Yes," Sylvia said, "I couldn't avoid that video going public. I prefer to remain behind the scenes."

"That's something the two of you have in common, isn't it?" Freddie asked. "You both work in the background with people who are in the limelight, so to speak."

"Yes, people behind the scenes tend to have longer careers," Noah said, glancing curiously at Sylvia. "Michael Fontaine is certainly making a splash in the public arena these days. Some of us in the Party think that we should ask him to lead us out of the wilderness we are in at the moment."

Freddie and Charlotte laughed, and so did George after a quick translation from Charlotte.

"Michael could do it, you know," Sylvia said. "He has the gift." She spoke quietly, smiling, and Noah nodded to himself.

Before Noah could respond, Freddie said, "Yes, no one should underestimate a preacher with a following that is growing a hundredfold every year."

"Charisma is in short supply in our current batch of politicians," Noah responded, with just an edge of bitterness.

"There is one exception, perhaps," Freddie said. "Your Sam Newbold is quite a talented man."

"Yes, that's right," Noah said briefly, but he didn't appear too enthusiastic, and Sylvia wondered whether Noah and Sam were allies or enemies. She was surprised that Freddie had mentioned Sam, and wondered where he was going with this line of talk.

"But can he be trusted?" Freddie asked.

Sylvia noticed that Charlotte and George had withdrawn from the conversation, chatting quietly in Mandarin to each other, looking absorbed in whatever they were discussing.

"I don't understand," Noah said. He wasn't the sort of person to be taken aback easily, Sylvia could see that. But it was obvious nonetheless that he was puzzled.

"I'm sure you won't mind me saying that your Sam Newbold suffers from a certain lack of judgement that affects his political career. He is unreliable, in the sense that he too easily forgets his friends, and the people who rely on him."

"Well, he is a politician, after all," Noah said easily.

"Apart from his many liaisons, both personal and political, which have been abandoned one after another, I am informed that in his youth he was quite the revolutionary?"

"Yes, in a sense," Noah said uncomfortably. "He was a student radical. Quite common during the Vietnam War, in this country. As a university student, young and headstrong."

"Certainly. I am also informed that he was a police spy at that time?"

"A rumour with no basis whatever," Noah said, looking taken aback.

Sylvia hadn't heard this rumour before, and she could tell that although Noah was still calm and polite, he might just show his teeth if Freddie persisted.

"I think that Sam Newbold's story illustrates how careful we must be in who we choose to associate with in life. In particular in business and politics. And who we depend on to lead us, especially in the higher realms of government."

"Politics requires a certain amount of ruthlessness," Noah said. "I'm sure that you understand that. Wouldn't you agree, Sylvia?"

"Yes, I do," Sylvia said. "But there are limits."

"Can you trust Sam Newbold?" Freddie asked Noah.

"I guess one day I'll find out," Noah said.

"Is it worth waiting for, Noah?" Freddie said. "There is an alternative, you know."

"What might that be?"

"To have a well paid role helping Michael Fontaine to enter politics. And, when the time comes, jump ship, as they say, and follow him into Federal politics. Please think about this. No need to answer now. For the initial twelve months, our terms are a quarter of a million dollars cash up front, and another quarter of a million at the end of the first year. With an option to renew."

Noah flushed a deep red, and stared at Freddie and Sylvia like a man hypnotized.

"What do you want?" he asked.

"We need your help, Noah," Freddie said. "My understanding is that the biggest threat to Michael on the Senate ticket will be Sam Newbold. If we are kept informed of the details of Sam's campaign, then we will have an advantage. You can leave the Labour Party and join GoodLord when you judge that it is the right time."

"OK. And what would happen when I join GoodLord?"

"You would have a leadership position on the GoodLord team. Well paid and influential. Michael will go far, as I am sure you are aware."

"What will be the next step if I accept? Here and now?" Noah asked.

"It is only a brief walk to my car, where the first instalment of cash is waiting for you to begin your new role. In total confidence."

Noah stood up unsteadily. "Let's go," he said, and Freddie walked out of the room with Noah, as Fong joined them for the one hundred metre walk to the car park.

As simple as that, Sylvia thought. All done in a matter of minutes. There was no point in Freddie going into detail with Noah, of course. The role he was meant to play was clear enough. An informant on what was happening in the Labour Party in the lead up to the Senate election, particularly in Sam Newbold's election campaign.

Sylvia had never been involved in an election before, and although she knew that Freddie Wu would be hiring the best advice in town, it had felt like a mountain to climb without a map or any climbing gear.

Now, however, with Labour's key numbers man effectively spiked, whether he could help Michael or not, there was a much better chance that they could win.

***

"Your husband hardly needs an election campaign, Mrs Fontaine," Noah Kowalski said to Sylvia. It was their first clandestine meeting to discuss the election, in one of Freddie Wu's safe houses, actually a luxury apartment near the docks. Alex, Michael's chauffeur and bodyguard, was posted at the door, to ensure her security.

"He can fill the MCG for a Sunday Gathering any time he likes," Noah added, "and broadcast it to the whole country. Far better than any election speech."

"Please call me Sylvia, Noah. And let's refer to my husband as Michael. I'm not an appendage to him."

"My apologies, Sylvia," Noah said smoothly.

"Let's get on with it."

"Certainly. As I was saying, Michael is a tremendous resource before we do a thing to help him. Probably we don't even need attack ads. Just gentle stuff urging the punters to vote for someone they can trust."

"And these ads can emphasize that he will serve as a Senator for everyone in the state, regardless of their beliefs?"

"Yes, of course."

"Will we have enough numbers?" Sylvia said. "I mean, however large Michael's audiences are, it's a fact that more people in Australia registered as 'no religion' in the last census than they did Christian."

"Yes, you're right," Noah said. "However, voting is a pretty fragmented business these days, especially in Senate elections. There are large numbers of candidates, and people are moving away from the two main parties in droves. So anyone with a concentrated block of votes, like Michael, stands a very good chance. Plus, he is an inclusive figure, well-liked across all demographics."

"What about Sam Newbold standing for the Senate?"

"Logically he should attract a large bloc of votes too. Although he failed in the election as Leader of the Opposition for Labour at state level, things might be better for him in a Senate election. He's popular, and he has a huge Party machine behind him."

"So Sam Newbold is the main threat to Michael's success in the election?" Sylvia asked.

"Yes, depending of course on how the rest of the field plays out," Noah said.

Of course, it was typical of Freddie Wu to identify their main strategic challenge at the outset. Sam Newbold was the only one of Michael's rivals for the Senate in Victoria to have even a flicker of charisma. She did not want to have Michael defeated in the election by a ghost from her past.

"Michael and Sam Newbold are neck and neck in the latest internal Party poll," Noah said. "It could be a tight finish."

Sylvia changed topics, concluding that whatever was to be done about Sam Newbold would have to be her own initiative. This was especially the case given that Noah was an unknown quantity, and was getting on well with Michael, good mates already in that Aussie tradition where males enjoyed a shared view of the world, talked football, had a beer together, and boasted about their insider status in the boys' club they inhabited in their daily work.

***

"I have a request to make, Anna," Sylvia said as they chatted in her office after lunch.

"Certainly," Anna said.

"I need your help in managing Noah Kowalski."

"What does that involve?" Anna sounded more curious than anything else, a promising sign.

"Although Noah is a valuable ally at the moment, he is also a potential threat in the future once he moves to GoodLord. We need to keep a close eye on him. Does that sound feasible to you?" Sylvia asked.

"Yes, of course."

Sylvia noticed that Anna revealed no discomfort about working against Noah, nor apparently any concerns about how challenging the task might be.

"I need you to manage surveillance on Noah, check who he is dealing with and so on. At least until he comes fully on board with GoodLord. He has a gambling problem, which made him susceptible to work with us for an offer of cash. Then again, that may make him susceptible to others as well. We need to be certain that he isn't playing both ends against the middle."

"No problem. Who does the actual surveillance?"

"We have a deal with Deten Inc. They have a security arm that we tap into."

"OK, good."

"So we're agreed. This is top secret and high priority. Of course it could be demanding. It will take more than surveillance, you'll need to get close to him, get a sense of what he's up to."

Anna smiled and nodded, looking completely relaxed.

"We'll begin by meeting with him and giving him a task," Sylvia said. Her aim was to provide a witness to the transaction with Noah, although Sylvia didn't spell this out. Noah had to feel answerable to GoodLord on more than the basis of his relationship to Michael, especially since Michael had a habit of taking it easy on people he liked. It was obvious that Noah was already getting to that stage of the game, something that had to be curtailed.

***

When Sylvia and Anna spoke to Noah he was a little flummoxed at first. "You want me to deliver a package to Sam Newbold?" he said, looking from Sylvia to Anna, and then back again.

They were sitting in Sylvia's city office on the twentieth floor, with a fine view of Albert Park Lake in the distance.

"That's right. It has to be delivered by hand. And it needs to be delivered to him by someone outside GoodLord, one of your offsiders, for instance. Someone you trust implicitly."

Noah looked taken aback, although this sort of thing could hardly be new to him.

"Why me?" he said.

"Obviously you are our main link to Sam Newbold. And you know him very well, not least because you are one of his main rivals. We need to work through intermediaries. Anna will be the link person at this end, which is why she's joined us for this meeting."

Noah glanced at Anna impatiently. "The whole thing is preposterous!"

"Noah, a very important package, containing information that will derail Sam Newbold's election campaign," Sylvia said.

"Not that old police spy rumour?"

"No, far worse than that. But the less said, the better."

"I see," he said after a moment, lips compressed. "OK, leave it to me."

"I'll hand over the package through Anna when the time is right. It will have to be delivered to a specific place at a specific time, no questions asked, in total confidence."

When Noah left Sylvia's office he was obviously struggling to contain his anger. It was always a dangerous proposition to make a pre-emptive strike against a powerful rival, especially to their face, rather than opting for a stab in the back. On the other hand, a warning shot across the bows could well be worth the trouble when dealing with someone as ambitious and ruthless as Noah Kowalski.

All that remained now was to talk to Sam Newbold.

***

It had been a long time since Sylvia had caught up with Sam. Although she still kept track of him, her commitment to GoodLord got in the way of direct contact. More recently political rivalry over the Senate election had further complicated her ambivalent attitude towards him.

However, now was the time to catch up with Sam. There was no sense in ignoring the threat to her future that he now posed. In any event, their relationship, however fragmented, had shadowed them both for a long time, with the lingering threat on both sides of revelations about Charlie Triado's death.

When she rang him he sounded surprised, but not hostile or uninterested.

"I hear a lot about your meteoric rise to fame," he said. "CEO of GoodLord, no less."

"And you are running for the Senate," Sylvia replied.

She could imagine his charming smile, and a tinge of smugness mingled with envy. She knew that Sam wouldn't appreciate competition from a former lover, no matter how long ago their relationship fizzled out. It had always struck her that he preferred his females to be in a subordinate position, and if not tied to the kitchen, then dependent on him in some essential way.

For herself, she felt beholden to him for his help at a time when she was still a lowly waitress. His recommendation of her to Star Finance had changed her life. On the other hand, Sam knew her darkest secret, and the only grip she had on the situation was the fact of his complicity in the police cover up of Charlie Triado's death.

"I'm tied down more than ever," she said, "and a lot of things can happen without much warning. That's the problem with a support role during an election."

"I understand," Sam said. "What can I do for you?" His tone was friendly and helpful, but still with the manner of the busy man with more important fish to fry.

"Is this line secure?" Sylvia asked.

"Yes, it is."

"I have some useful information for you." she said. "A very interesting video."

"Showing what?"

"A certain person caught in a compromising situation. Compromising enough to destroy him. Your election would be guaranteed if it became public."

After a moment's silence Sam said, "Ah, blackmail. A very dangerous game."

"Yes, and it can be very rewarding. I have alternatives I want to pursue. And I want payback before I do."

"I see. Interesting. How do I gain possession of this fascinating piece of information?"

"In person. It will most definitely destroy him if it gets out."

"Why not email it to me?"

"It's too hot for anyone else to handle. This has to be completely secure."

"And how do you know it's for real?"

"You'll have to take my word for it."

"What's your price?"

"It's free. As I said, it's a matter of payback."

There was a long silence.

"So, when and where?" Sam asked.

"I'll ring you," Sylvia said, then went to the office kitchen and placed her burner phone in the microwave on "reheat" for a few moments before throwing it in the rubbish bin.

CHAPTER 10

HARRY

It's coming up to dusk but I leave my headlights off, side lights only. A hot evening in Melbourne, aircon thrumming, the extreme heat kicking in even though it's still spring, as the years of drought continue.

I double-check the satnav for my location, confirming that I am close to my destination, a layby alongside Albert Park Lake, only a couple of kilometres away from the central business district. A quiet spot, free of surveillance cameras. Why Sam Newbold would agree to a meeting like this is beyond me, but as usual I'm following Noah's orders to the letter, no questions asked.

"He'll be in a white Ford," Noah says to me. "And he'll be alone. Stop about fifty metres from his car, wait till he hops out so that you can identify him for sure, you give him this package. Don't talk to him. You both return to your cars, drive off. Job done."

"What's in the package?"

"I don't know. It's a message from upstairs that we have to pass on. So don't open it."

Noah taps the small package on his desk with his forefinger, holding my gaze, then hands it to me. Strange behaviour for a guy who usually barks his orders over his shoulder on his way out of the office for a cigarette.

God knows what "a message from upstairs" means in this context. Not many people were "upstairs" from Noah in the Party, and why send a secret message via Noah?

Now the package is sitting on the passenger seat beside me. It's one of those little boxes you used to be able to buy from the Post Office to send off videos by snail mail. It's covered in brown paper, all sticky-taped up, nothing written on it.

Whatever it contains, it's not very heavy, and you can't feel what's in it because of the cardboard it's wrapped in. A wad of one hundred dollar bills? A small notebook? Uncut diamonds? Who knows?

OK, so here I am. I can see the white Ford I'm looking for parked in this layby. I park close to the road under a tree, streaks of sunset fading behind the city buildings, all lit up in the near distance across the lake.

I get out of the car, package in hand, trying to look casual as the heat hits me and instantly I begin to sweat. Sam Newbold climbs out of his car, and walks towards me. I recognize Sam from his TV appearances, wearing a nice pair of suit pants, white shirt without a tie, sleeves rolled up, his wavy silver hair a trademark feature of a mature charismatic politician. I haven't been up close to him in person since we were both student activists back in the day, and he is looking at me curiously. Yes, he looks his age, a few years older than me, but so do I. He still has that swagger, even in these dubious circumstances.

I silently hold out the package to him, but he just keeps looking at me.

"Don't I know you? What are you doing here?" Sam says, staring at me uncomprehendingly. Good memory, or maybe he's caught sight of me in passing around the traps. Doubtful, though. Who the hell is he expecting?

"Take it," I say gruffly, pushing the package at him again. He takes it and I turn back to my car abruptly, leaving him standing there.

I hear him walk off over the gravel, and glance over my shoulder. He is standing by his car opening the package. I take a few steps more, but then I hear a vehicle engine. A black SUV, lights off in the dim twilight, eases into the layby. Bad timing, but it's a public place, no harm done. However, the SUV accelerates with a spray of gravel, turning the headlights on to full beam.

Sam turns his head at the sound, one hand raised to shield his eyes from the glare of the headlights. The SUV lurches forward, picking up speed instantly and swerves towards Sam, slamming him against his car.

The SUV keeps going, fishtailing away in the gravel, leaving Sam sprawled on the ground, and accelerates for the exit. The driver is a blur behind darkened privacy glass, lights now off, and I can't see the number plate.

I run over to Sam's car and kneel beside him. He is sprawled awkwardly on his back, arms limp beside his body, head thrown back, legs twisted beneath him, one shoe on the ground in a pool of blood. The package is lying on the ground, torn open and half empty, white powder splashed about on the gravel as well as on his clothes.

Blood is seeping from a gash on Sam's head, down his neck and onto his white shirt, and I can't bring myself to look more closely at his legs. His eyes are open, but he doesn't blink and there is no sign of him breathing. I should check his pulse to be certain, but I don't.

I do the only thing I can do; run back to my car, start the engine, trying to stay calm and driving slowly away alongside the lake, around to the city side. No one is following me, so I switch on the car lights after a couple of hundred metres. Near St

Kilda junction, I'm still struggling for breath and my hands are shaking. I stop and take the burner phone out of the glovebox, draw several deep breaths, check the satnav for Sam's precise location and disguise my voice to ring for an ambulance. Then switch the phone off.

I start driving, and throw the burner phone out the window, and see it clatter into the gutter in the rear view mirror. I desperately want to know what was in the package. It looked like drugs, or laundry powder when you pour it into the washing machine. Maybe talcum powder. But who would send laundry powder or talcum powder to a prominent politician? So it had to be drugs, maybe cocaine. I know nothing about drugs, but shoving white powder up your nose is all the rage, apparently, and maybe Sam was into it?

I drive for a few blocks, still shaking like a leaf, then pull over to try and think. Whoever did this is not messing around, that's obvious. Question is, would they be after me? If they were, they would have bumped me off at the same time, while I was standing there in shock, a potential witness, an easy target. But they didn't. So maybe it's reasonably safe to assume they won't follow up. Although for all I know a professional hitman will have no qualms in following up any old time it suits him. Even an amateur. I have no fucking idea.

Somehow somebody, who knows who, followed me to the rendezvous. Or more likely, come to think of it, they followed Sam. Didn't need to know anything about me or any package. Just needed a clear run at the target in a quiet spot. Who is it? And what is Noah's role in all this? He gave me the package, obviously he knows more than he lets on.

I take a deep breath, sweating despite the car aircon, and drive carefully in a zigzag through the back streets of town. A detour might be in order so that I arrive home from a different direction. Paranoia is setting in.

I park outside our house, and leave a brief urgent message for Noah's voicemail. I'm betting he'll ring me back within the hour.

***

Noah sounds as shocked as I am by Sam Newbold's death when we talk on the phone. The next day we meet in my office to talk things over in more detail.

"It's fucking unbelievable," Noah says. He's looking more dishevelled than ever, and is pulling furiously on his cigarette. "What the hell is going on? Who would want to kill Sam Newbold?"

"I don't know. Like I said on the phone, the SUV appeared out of nowhere. It was dark, the headlights were switched on full beam, I couldn't see inside it."

"Yeah, well. Tell no one about it. What happened to the package?"

"Sam opened it," I say. "White powder was spilt on his clothes, on the ground."

"Shit!" Noah says. "You didn't clean it up?"

"Impossible. It was all over the place."

"Shit!" he says again.

"Will this incriminate us in any way?" I ask him, but he just grimaces, not answering.

"We have to move on, Harry. Somehow. Business as usual. Stick to our usual routines. The police appear to have no leads, at least as far as I can tell from the news. And no witnesses. It's being billed as a hit-and-run accident."

"All to the good," I say. "And there's no CCTV anywhere in that area, and very little through traffic."

We are talking in my Lygon Street office because it's a good place for confidential conversations, with dim old-fashioned corridors, no open plan spaces whatever, and no glassed-wall offices like Noah's fancy digs at The Secretariat.

Noah is standing at the window, looking out through a gap in the venetian blinds. It's a nice view of Lygon Street, you can just see my favourite café down the road, but remembering Sam Newbold killed right in front of me, I don't feel like looking at it.

Noah stays silent, fiddling distractedly with his smartphone. I don't bother asking him any more questions. But I ask myself. Who would send Sam a package of cocaine? To what extent is Noah involved? Whoever is responsible, the package must have been some sort of bait, to draw Sam to an isolated spot.

All politicians have enemies, Sam Newbold more than most. And the person most likely to benefit from Sam's death is Michael Fontaine, his main rival in the election. But surely no one would go that far to win an election?

***

The news is dominated by speculation about Sam's death, the press and TV lingering on the gory details. The cocaine in the package hasn't been mentioned yet, but that is surely just a matter of time.

Getting to sleep is difficult, night after night. I stay wide awake and just lie there, staring at the ceiling, listening to Rita's rhythmical breathing. She can sleep through a thunderstorm, whereas I have always been a light sleeper. Now the slightest noise wakes me up.

Seeing Sam Newbold's bloody corpse is more than I can handle. I haven't seen a corpse close up before, let alone the violence that caused it. Funerals don't count; a dead body of someone you know lying in a coffin in a funeral parlour wearing their best clothes is so unreal, all perfect and still like a wax model, you might as well be in a movie. All I have ever seen of death out in the open is a body lying on the ground beside a crashed car, a small crowd standing around staring at it. Just a brief glimpse as I drive past. That is enough.

My dreams are vivid, but it's not the images that concern me so much, it's the feeling of stark terror re-lived as I dream, more intense than I can remember for the actual half a minute I stood there in shock looking at Sam's body before I made a run for it.

I'm left feeling ragged in the mornings, and my bad moods and irritation start to wear Rita down. There is no way I can tell her why I am such a mess, that I was actually on the scene when Sam died.

I'm going through a work crisis, I tell her. Sam's death is a shock, I say. True enough, but nothing that goes even half way to explaining the angst that must be radiating from me so that it's as tangible as a scream in the dark.

To make matters worse, within forty eight hours of Sam's death, the news breaks in the tabloid press alleging that he has recently been implicated in a police investigation into huge donations made by Chinese nationals to Australian political parties. And a little later, the headlines scream "cocaine found on hit-and-run politician," adding yet more murky detail to the whole catastrophe.

I have endless baffled conversations with Noah Kowalski, by now becoming agitated, something unusual for him. I've seen him angry plenty of times, but I'm not accustomed to seeing outright fear on his face.

We talk pointlessly about what the hell is going on, but we get nowhere and decide to shove Sam's murder under the carpet with everything else we don't talk about. Try to stay focused on appearing completely ignorant, we say to each other, especially if any police enquiries came our way. Surely there are enough politicians and party hacks involved in hoovering up donations from Chinese donors to keep the authorities playing catchup for the next decade. But the added mess of Sam's murder, and his supposed involvement in drugs and dirty money, tilts the whole thing out of balance.

Given all the fuss, we reason that we should keep our heads down. This is easier for me than for Noah. He is well known in political circles, hobnobbing with the leaders who are constantly in the news, whereas I am an anonymous stringer, a bit like a freelance journalist selling his wares to established news media. Except that my name never appears in print. Even the office I use is rented from a union that uses various business names to rent property, and my anonymous Camry is leased in the name of God knows what consultancy funded by some outfit that only exists on paper.

***

Once the shock of Sam's death and the initial news media fuss has passed, I wonder why Neil Bautervich hasn't given me a heads-up on the investigation into political donations, if in fact it really exists. I break protocol and ring him outside the usual schedule, and arrange to meet him for the umpteenth time in Poynton's Pub, handy close by.

He's as vague as ever when we meet up for a beer, and I ask him what is going on. Why all this nonsense in the news about Sam and political donations?

"We're throwing the dog a bone," he says. "It's an opportune move, to flag the donations problem, and we need a suspect who won't be appearing in TV interviews."

"You mean Sam Newbold? Because he's dead," I say, "and he's not around to contradict you. And you've got the added issue of drugs to muddy the waters."

"Exactly. I see that your gift for calling a spade a shovel hasn't left you," Neil mutters. "Don't worry, we can keep you out of any investigations. So long as you don't leave any paperwork lying around."

"There's no paper trail. And I'm hired at third or fourth hand by totally unrelated entities."

"That's what you need," Neil says, sarcasm dripping from every word. "Unrelated entities will save your arse every time."

Presumably, whoever Neil works for wants to expose the whole shady business of Chinese money buying favours in Australian politics, while managing to avoid the fallout from a prominent politician like Sam Newbold defending himself endlessly in the news. Then they'll appoint some alphabet soup investigative body, ABBD or whatever, to probe into what is happening and come up with convenient findings. And Neil goes on to confirm exactly that.

"Given the involvement of so many politicians in all aspects of the huge amounts of Chinese money flowing into Australia," Neil says, "there'll be a lot of noise and smoke, with no one being charged with anything much, unless they can find a sacrificial lamb. Someone who for some reason is out of favour with people who matter. Being anonymous is a lifesaver at times like this. So stay with it. Keep your head down. The real issues are being handled in secret."

Neil is right. ABBD makes several vague announcements over a few days or so, then falls silent. They also manage to even things up, in terms of political loyalties, with more news reports on China's influence, this time in Sydney politics, on the conservative side of the game. Again, the allegations conveniently involve someone who won't talk, a senior Coalition official who has died recently, this time from a heart attack.

Just to be sure, Noah and I spend a lot of time burying all the evidence we can as fast as possible. We salt away large sums of cash, and we change our routines so as to cover our tracks, including no more meetings with our donors in Chinese restaurants.

Over time we've become far too relaxed about the whole damn business. While we want to keep the donor pipeline open, we slow down our funding activity for the time being and wait to see what will happen. The way things are going, at best I could be looking down the barrel of early retirement.

***

"What the hell is going on?" Ben Reilly says. "Sam Newbold killed in a hit-and-run, God help us. Involved in a dodgy donations racket, found dead with drugs scattered around him. And Michael Fontaine now certain to be elected to the Senate!"

Ben takes off his glasses and rubs his eyes, a picture of despair. It's disconcerting to see an incorrigible optimist in such a bad way. Michael Fontaine's rise to fame is no surprise to me, but most of the Labour Party seem to be stunned by it.

We're having lunch in Café Lorenzo in Carlton, two veterans of so-called Left wing politics, greying hair in Ben's case, bald as a billiard ball in mine. I've reached the stage where the university students sitting at another table, all gazing at their iPhones while they chat and show each other their screens, look impossibly young. I have to resist the urge to reminisce about how much better Café Lorenzo was in the old days, which isn't true anyway, it's much smarter now, in keeping with the gentrification of Lygon Street and the whole of Carlton. I don't miss 1970's inner-city grunge, that was just rich kids slumming it. The coffee is much better these days too, no doubt about that.

I don't answer Ben's rhetorical question about the reasons for the paradigm shift in federal politics. Any way you look at it, the so-called political mainstream is now dead in the water.

"We've been outplayed by complete novices!" Ben adds. "By Michael Fontaine, of all people."

So we sit there gloomily, Ben hunched over his coffee, a tall gangle of a man who can barely fit his long legs under the table.

Things are so bad, he has barely touched his tortellini with mushrooms. Not a good sign. Nothing stops me eating. I've finished my main course and I'm considering some zabaglione, but now doesn't seem like a good time to order.

We're feeling like ageing racehorses marked down for the knacker's yard, risible self pity from two affluent old men who still get to do pretty much what they like and are well paid for it. Self pity, like schadenfreude, is a deep well to draw from, and very satisfying too.

It's a fact that no one in the main parties knows what to do about GoodLord Inc. In the early stages of the political shift that is now upon us, no one could imagine the full extent of what was coming. Conventional politicians stood around gawping slack-jawed while Michael Fontaine ate their lunch. I enjoyed watching it happen, while feeling nervous about the overall consequences.

Michael Fontaine represents perfectly the brave new world of unstinted possibilities, the sort you only have to reach out for to be rewarded instantly, because you deserve it, in a time full of uncertain dangers and cruel twists of fate.

***

Neil Bautervich wants to see me again to give me an update. Meeting with him these days is like going to the dentist when I was a kid, painful anticipation followed by painful recollection.

"Your situation over the Sam Newbold business is going downhill," Neil says morosely.

At least our meeting has been upgraded to a bar in an expensive hotel in Collins Street in the city. I'm not sure if that is a good thing or not. Maybe Neil's mysterious masters stretch the expense account a little when they are about to hang you out to dry, maybe offer you a prison sentence rather than being shot at dawn. Farewell drinks, so to speak.

We're tucked away in a private corner with a nice view over the city to the Dandenong Ranges. Neil orders gin and tonics because of the hot weather, although the aircon wafting over us is chilly.

"My situation is going downhill? What the hell does that mean?" I say. "No one saw us. Except for the SUV driver, and they won't be coming forward. There was nothing I could do about the drugs spilt all over the place after Sam was hit."

"Yes, I know. But we can only obstruct the police so far, and no further," Neil says. "Your confidential report on Sam Newman for Noah Kowalski has surfaced, and fingers are pointing at you as having a role in Newbold's demise."

"I'm just the investigator," I protest. "There's no benefit to me in getting rid of Sam."

"It doesn't necessarily look that way," Neil says. "The conspiracy against Sam Newbold is looking very murky to some of my colleagues."

"That's ridiculous."

"It's like this," Neil says. "There's a task force working on Chinese influence in Australian politics, mostly a showcase sort of thing, for public benefit. But behind that, there's some serious cooperation in play between the major agencies. And the Sam Newbold murder case is seen by the agencies as an important link between key figures involved in serious national security issues. Too many coincidences."

Neil stops and looks at me, as though he has just revealed the whereabouts of buried treasure.

"What fucking coincidences?" I say. "Where do I come into all this?"

"Well, your role in the Sam Newbold case has leaked out. The whole situation is almost a replay of how you stumbled into Sam Newbold's little Maoist group back in the day when he made his start in politics. Now you're caught up in how it came to an end. Suspicious." Then Neil paused. "And there's more," he added with a frown.

"What's that?"

"We think that Sam might have been killed by a group of influential Chinese players," he says. "In an effort to ensure that Michael Fontaine can gain entry to Federal politics. A Machiavellian decision supporting GoodLord. With Noah Kowalski and you as party to all that."

"How do you connect me to GoodLord through Noah?" I say. "The Labour Party needed Sam to win that election. Which Noah supported."

"Yes, I believe you. All true. However, Noah Kowalski has been working for GoodLord since the election was called. Michael Fontaine hired him as a consultant some time ago. Basically as an informer on what Sam Newbold's election campaign was doing. So your connection to Kowalski is a bad look."

"You are fucking kidding me!"

"Not at all," Neil says. "We have surveillance footage of Noah Kowalski meeting with Charlotte Hung and Freddie Wu at a restaurant, and being paid off. We also have reports of Noah meeting regularly with GoodLord staff, and Fontaine's wife, at various locations, including their city office."

"I don't believe you," I say, almost choking.

"Why not?" Neil says coldly. "Politicians change parties during a crisis. At the moment the so-called major parties in this country are experiencing an unprecedented decline. Think about it. And, of course, Noah Kowalski has his gambling debts to consider. Upwards of six figures. The more money he makes, the bigger the bets he lays down."

Neil is right. It's just that I see Noah as a classic Labour diehard, someone who would go down with the ship.

"OK, OK. Now what?"

"We need the clearest picture possible of what GoodLord is up to. Who is funding them, what their strategy is."

"What about finding out who killed Sam Newbold?" I say.

"That's a job for the police. There's no doubt that the GoodLord outfit killed Sam Newbold for political reasons."

Neil sits looking at me with a strange expression on his face.

"What? Why are you telling me all this?" I say.

Usually he tells me bugger all. The last time he gave me anything resembling a briefing, I ended up reporting to him about Charlotte Hung and the political donations that flowed from her and through me to Noah Kowalski. That changed the course of my life, mostly in a good way. Now I have cause to regret it.

"The political donations associated with Charlotte Hung and her circle lead us to wonder what part GoodLord and Michael Fontaine are playing in the growing influence of China in Australian politics. It is developing dangerous tendencies."

"What dangerous tendencies?" I ask.

"Obviously a willingness to assassinate an Australian politician in an effort to assist their preferred candidate. That would make Michael Fontaine the stooge of a foreign government."

Neil says this with some emotion, unusual for him.

"No solid proof, though," I say.

"That's where you come in," Neil says.

"Sounds dangerous to me," I say. "Maybe you're reading too much into Sam's death. There could be all sorts of reasons."

"No, very unlikely. The murder of Sam Newbold was definitely done for political reasons. By someone who knew Sam Newbold would be there to collect that package, and managed to intercept him and kill him. The drugs are just a distraction."

"But they could have followed Sam," I say.

"No. We monitored him on CCTV all the way to the Albert Park entrance, where it cut out, and no one followed him. There was no tracking device on his car, and no drones in the area. Plus he had a burner phone, new that day, and they wouldn't be able to track his phone either."

"OK. What now?" I ask.

"For starters, we will be placing surveillance on the key players at GoodLord, such as Noah Kowalski and Sylvia Fontaine. But we also need someone actually on the spot to see what's happening. We want you to infiltrate GoodLord and report back to us. We know that Noah Kowalski is involved with GoodLord, but we need specific evidence of what he's up to."

"Infiltrate? No way," I say. "No way."

"The alternative, unfortunately," Neil says, "and this comes from on high, is that you will be charged with conspiracy to murder."

"How the hell would I infiltrate GoodLord?" I ask him. "Sign on as a member? I'd be lost in the crowd."

"We're assuming Kowalski will take you with him when he moves to GoodLord. You've been his right arm where dealings with the Chinese are concerned."

"The thing is, my work for him won't be needed once he shifts to GoodLord," I say.

"Nothing's guaranteed, of course. But it would make sense for him to build his own team with his own people. And who else would he take with him from the Labour Party but you?"

"Fair enough. But why would I want to move to GoodLord with him?"

"Noah knows you've got no interest in politics, as such. In other words, you could play your role within any party. Much like the consultant you claim to be on your income tax forms. Just continue your so-called consultancy role, doing his dirty work for him."

"Thanks very much."

"You're a high-value informant, Harry. Don't forget that. We appreciate it."

"And that means what? A bonus?"

"You'll be rolling in cash in GoodLord. Executive staff there all live like kings."

"Good to hear that religion pays well," I say.

CHAPTER 11

SYLVIA

Barney Hanson, the new Prime Minister, was clearly a small-minded ignoramus who had never progressed beyond the politics of his local pub. This meant, of course, that he was adored by a loud minority of like-minded citizens sharing his crimped view of the world.

At least Hanson was honest in expressing his opinions, and could not be swayed to change them to win more votes. However, to Sylvia's mind this was a fatal flaw in any politician, and made his downfall inevitable.

The overall election results had produced a potpourri of minor parties and independents, with no single party winning the numbers to make a majority. With Sam Newbold out of the way, Michael had an armchair ride into the Senate, winning his seat by a comfortable margin, one of the many new Independents to be elected.

"Terrible news about Sam Newbold. Much as it's good news for my election campaign, it's an awful way to go. And not exactly a fair win," Michael said to Sylvia when they were discussing the news of Sam's death.

"Yes, although there were drugs involved, apparently. Maybe he was meeting his drug dealer and things went wrong," she said.

Sylvia hadn't felt any particular animosity towards Sam Newbold. Their relationship when she was young had been mutually beneficial, and although Sam was arrogant and unthinking, he was also good company and someone who was always willing to help her out. She just didn't feature seriously in any of his plans for the future, and she could not rely on him long term. Not like Freddie Wu. And when it came to the threat that Sam posed to Michael's election to the Senate, then the end justifies the means, and Sam had to go.

After the election, Michael was still agonizing over his lucky break.

"The whole business of Sam's death makes me feel a bit guilty about winning the election."

"You would have won anyway," Sylvia said firmly, and Michael nodded in agreement. Sylvia could see that he would soon get over his guilty feelings, what with all the glory heaped on him in the media for his rise to national politics.

Freddie's reaction to Sam's death was quite different to Michael's, of course.

"I didn't realize that you were going to resolve the issue so forcefully," he said to Sylvia.

"So you assume that I was responsible?" Sylvia said.

"Who else?" Freddie smiled. "A very effective solution. High risk, though."

"I've had nothing to do with Sam for a long time, so there is no obvious connection."

"Apart from the benefit to Michael's bid for the Senate."

"Yes, of course, but nothing like this has happened in Australian politics before, at least as public knowledge. And let's face it, the police aren't exactly well known for their vivid imaginations."

"No, quite true. A great gamble, and a successful one. Congratulations."

***

Now was the time to be looking forward, not back. Obviously the days of the so-called major political parties were over, providing perfect conditions for a charismatic independent politician like Michael Fontaine to come into his own, once PM Hanson was out of the way.

A bonus was the politics of tight corners that came with the election of a minority Government, hanging onto a razor thin majority by its fingertips. Sylvia enjoyed all the plotting and manoeuvring, even if it did mean flying between Melbourne and Canberra to attend the sittings of the Senate in the federal capital. Sylvia observed parliamentary debates from the gallery, amazed by the atmosphere of adolescent conflict, like a brawl at an out of control drunken party thrown by teenagers while their parents were away for the weekend.

It was interesting watching the problems Barney Hanson had in making the shift from self-appointed lone champion of the underdog to Prime Minister of the entire country. Was he even aware of what was required? He simply could not let go of his parish pump style of imprecation and complaint, flitting from one irrelevant grievance to another, oblivious to the fact that it was now his job to solve problems, not complain about them at the top of his voice. He was like the captain of a ship ranting about the brass doorknobs needing a polish while the ship was sinking.

"All we have to do is back Hanson into a corner and keep him there," Sylvia said to Michael. "He'll soon be totally helpless, then he'll have to resign."

Michael chuckled, nodding his head. "Yes, poor old Barney can't be getting much sleep these days. There's no one he can trust, least of all the people in his own party. And there's only a handful of them at that."

When the Senate was sitting Sylvia and Michael spent most of their spare time in their Canberra apartment plotting their next moves. Apart from boozy parties with the usual crowd of politicians with their feral egos and ferocious lobbying of each other, journalists, powerful rent-seekers and any other audience they could corner, there was little else to do.

"Hanson might be on his last gasp," Sylvia said to Fontaine, "but it's better to leave him swinging in the wind for a little while longer. That will make our task easier." The task was, of course, taking over the Prime Ministership, with Noah favouring an alliance with another party to strengthen their hand.

Sylvia was totally opposed to alliances of any kind. However, in spite of their differences, face-to-face contact with Noah worked quite well, no doubt because he now understood Sylvia's grip on the Fontaine Government.

Nothing further had been said between Sylvia and Noah about the envelope delivered to Sam Newbold. It appeared that Noah felt complicit in Sam's death, and would prefer the whole issue to be buried forever. However, Sylvia remained suspicious of Noah's loyalty to GoodLord, and kept a close eye on Anna Kalajian's surveillance reports.

"Noah cycles through a steady routine according to the surveillance," Anna said. "Long work hours, time in the pub and on the racetrack, activities with his wife and kids, and occasional visits to a girlfriend on the other side of town."

"Nothing suspicious then?" Sylvia said.

"Not so far. Large gambling debts, though."

"Keep the surveillance going. Send some of our people into his house when everyone's out, check for notebooks, laptops etcetera. Find out who he owes money to."

Sylvia still did not trust Noah, whatever the lack of evidence.

***

While religion was their cornerstone, Sylvia ensured that GoodLord welcomed everyone regardless of their beliefs or lack of them, and criticized no individuals and no rival groups, keeping their attacks on the Hanson Government focussed on specific issues threatening Michael's rise to power.

GoodLord was Christian, of course, but it was the religion of the Jesus who cares for everyone, not a religion that seeks to privilege and exclude. That was Michael's modus operandi, reflecting his naive trust in people, and Sylvia insisted that they kept to the mantra of "come one, come all," a message that distinguished them from all other religious groups.

It was a simple message, couched in everyday language. Established religions were promised total tolerance with Michael Fontaine as their Senator in Canberra, together with the amorphous mass of GoodLord Inc members and fellow travellers.

These fellow travellers were an important component of Sylvia's plan, ensuring the support of people who were not members of the GoodLord congregation, but who accepted that Michael Fontaine was obviously a good man with every citizen's welfare close to his heart. He would force the privileged elite in Canberra to do the right thing.

In Sylvia's opinion, Canberra and its institutions were as artificial as the so-called democracy it was meant to represent, and she regarded the wildfires threatening Canberra as a golden opportunity. In the end, it was simply a matter of choosing the right moment.

***

All that lay between the approaching fires and the Houses of Parliament, Sylvia told Michael, was a few ornamental lakes and an under-resourced fire brigade.

Little thought had been given to environmental threats by the architects of Canberra back in the 1920s. It was a privileged enclave, a designer capital built to house Australia's federal politicians in the equivalent of a gated community.

"We need to be on standby," Sylvia said. "When those fires hit, it will take a miracle to escape." Michael nodded, seemingly at a loss to comprehend the threat.

Freddie Wu was delighted with the emerging crisis. "The situation in Canberra is panning out just as we discussed, Sylvia," he said over breakfast when they met in Freddie's apartment in Melbourne. "The crisis we need has arrived. We must plan carefully."

"The situation with the fires is chaotic," Sylvia said. "No one knows what to do. In the end, the politicians will run for the exits, with Barney Hanson leading the way. There is no plan of action to deal with the fires or even where to reconvene Parliament and the Senate in a national emergency, if Canberra is compromised."

"Typical politicians," Freddie said. "Of course, with the whole country on fire, there is the basic issue of where to run to. Very difficult, especially as these fires start without warning, anywhere and everywhere."

"Melbourne is safest, it seems to me. It's simply a matter of relocating the federal parliament to Melbourne," Sylvia said. She finished her grapefruit, and poured more coffee. "Victoria's Houses of Parliament are only a couple of kilometres from both the Yarra river and Port Phillip Bay. Every politician could easily exit Parliament and reach a safe place in a matter of minutes."

"But of course, Parliament here in Melbourne is filled with State politicians," Freddie said.

"Yes," Sylvia said, "but at the moment they are on recess for several weeks as Christmas approaches, followed by annual holidays. They don't even bother to look as though they are making an effort. And there is no particular need to call them back."

"I see what you mean."

Freddie paced quietly up and down the bedroom, pausing now and again to gaze at their view of the bay. "An ideal location," he murmured.

"Yes, Sylvia said. "Parliament House in Melbourne is also the perfect place to hold a Gathering. Which could install Michael as Prime Minister by consent. GoodLord members could fill the entire CBD of Melbourne. A hundred thousand members is all it would take. A popular vote, endorsed all over the country. Perhaps in simultaneous Gatherings. And we can do all that at the drop of a hat. We could govern the country with a National Cabinet. State Governments are a waste of time and money anyway. And I think that the declaration of a National Emergency would give us the opportunity to put everything up for grabs. There won't be much opposition from Barney Hanson. He's the same as any other rabble rouser, all mouth and no trousers, as my father would say."

"Sylvia, I knew from the first time we met that you would go far," Freddie said. "Didn't I say that to you?"

"Yes, you did."

"What about the composition of your National Cabinet? You are staying in the wings, I take it?

"Yes."

"And you have Noah Kowalski ready to take up a role in the Cabinet?" Freddie asked.

"Yes, as Minister for National Security and Home Affairs," Sylvia said.

"Although Noah hasn't been voted into Parliament, of course," Freddie said.

"The new National Emergency regulations will fix that problem, and any other issues that get in the way."

"Excellent."

***

It was a high-risk proposition to dissolve the current Houses of Parliament and "elect" Michael by popular consent. Not least of the problems would be getting Michael to agree. Any important decision was difficult for him to arrive at, let alone one as big as this.

Nonetheless, Sylvia knew that an existential crisis was about to envelop the whole country, and anyone with a bold plan that held out the possibility of survival would win the day. GoodLord Inc had the national organization, backed up with the resources, to get the job done. There was nothing else in Australia to match it.

Even more importantly, GoodLord also had the support of large numbers of the police and the army, having made law and order the keystone of Michael's offer of a safe and secure future for everyone, including the promise of a significant increase in funding.

And Freddie Wu was already in the good graces of the Governor General, Dame Mona Lippi, former lawyer and judge, someone who had extensive networks in the institutions of government and law across the country.

"The minute Barney Hanson bolts for safety back to his Gold Coast mansion, we must be ready to move with a proposal to Dame Mona for the appointment of Michael as interim Prime Minister," Sylvia said to Freddie. "And I will need your help to convince Dame Mona that this is the right way to go."

"Absolutely," Freddie said. "And I have extra funds at your disposal for anything that stretches the GoodLord budget," he said. "My entire network will give you unlimited support. Their lobbyists can go into action tomorrow," he added. "And don't forget that Zelda Freestone is a keen supporter of GoodLord, even though she hasn't gone public yet."

"A public pledge of support from Zelda would be timely," Sylvia said.

"No problem."

***

In Canberra later that week, Sylvia and Michael stood at their apartment window watching the sky filling with smoke, the acrid smell overcoming the air conditioning. The horizon was alight with flames streaming up into the sky, reminiscent of the recent disastrous megafires all along the east coast.

"Good God!" Michael said, and Sylvia could hear the fear in his voice.

They watched the TV news together, showing the roads blocked with panicked families trying to escape in every direction, except that Canberra was ringed with intense bushfires, now burning out of control across the whole city, and there was nowhere to go.

"We'll be OK," Sylvia said to Michael, as he paced up and down the apartment, looking occasionally out the window at the plumes of smoke swirling past their windows.

Cars were bumper to bumper on the roads to the airport, despite announcements that it was closed to the public. Freddie had foreseen this problem, arranging with Zelda Freestone to send two helicopters to the grounds of Parliament to rescue Sylvia and Michael with their staff.

"I would send my own copters, but it would be more discreet to use Zelda's. A foreign national like myself would draw unwanted attention to Michael," he said to Sylvia.

Their helicopter flight out of Canberra was a nightmare of smoke that obliterated the horizon, quick snatches of burning houses and trees visible below them, with flames reaching up to incredible heights. Then merciful release as they skimmed over as yet untouched countryside on the way to Sydney airport.

The helicopter pounded noisily along, such a blast of sound that they didn't attempt talking to each other until they landed.

"Thank God," Michael groaned when they arrived, and Sylvia half expected him to fall on his knees on the tarmac in a prayer of thanks.

Smoke was on the horizon in Sydney too, and Sylvia felt relieved when they transferred to the GoodLord jet and continued on to Melbourne. God knows how other people without their resources were coping, but at this stage it was everyone for themselves. There was still no sign of an organized response to the chaos around them.

Once in Melbourne, Sylvia and Michael were able to reach their house without any problems. While megafires were threatening the northern outer suburbs, they had been stopped from crossing the ring road. From the comfort of their lounge room they could watch the disaster unfolding in Canberra on TV, with the Houses of Parliament burned to the ground, and the Government in total disarray.

Prime Minister Hanson disappeared from view, his shaky alliances decimated, and his small group of parliamentarians reduced to just two people, himself and a lone Senator from the Northern Territory.

***

Escape from Canberra was a relief, but now the question was, what next? Communications were patchy, but Sylvia was able to launch their grand plan to hold simultaneous Gatherings of the congregation across the country at short notice.

Luckily, Dame Mona was based in Melbourne, her hometown, and she invited Michael and Sylvia to her mansion in Toorak in response to calls for an urgent course of action from Zelda Freestone and her group of business magnates, backed by the military, a chorus of lobbyists and the news media.

"Now is the time to be decisive; we can't do things by halves. We need to abolish the Lower House of Federal Parliament, and establish a National Cabinet," Sylvia said to Michael. "It's something the entire population will support."

Michael looked uneasy, but the prospect of becoming Prime Minister in the near future soothed any doubts, aided by Freddie Wu's counsel on the need for "lean and mean" Government in times of emergency.

"A National Cabinet is a wonderful idea," Freddie said. "It's the equivalent of a War Cabinet. Let's face it, there's no time to indulge in wide-ranging debates. This crisis, as you have said yourself, Michael, needs decisive action. Taken with a consensus of dedicated leaders. And without all the pork barrelling on behalf of this interest group or that."

"Yes, I agree," Michael said, reassured by Freddie's wide knowledge of politics and world affairs.

***

Dame Mona was most accommodating as they sat down for crisis discussions, their only witness her private secretary, who sat to one side of them taking notes.

"The need for urgent action is very clear, Senator Fontaine," she said. "And in fact there are precedents for temporary measures involving exactly the sort of 'National Cabinet' that you propose. Gough Whitlam, for example, began his term of office in 1972 with two or three Ministers, I believe."

"Yes, Dame Mona," Michael replied. "And once things return to normal, we can of course review my interim Prime Ministership in the clear light of day, with a view to returning to the standard practice established by convention and tradition."

These words rolled off Michael's tongue very smoothly, not surprising considering that he had practised them with Sylvia before the appointment with the Governor General.

Sylvia smiled beside him as they sat opposite Dame Mona in exquisite Regency chairs at her residence in Toorak. A servant had deposited cups of coffee on a low table between them, and Sylvia sat quietly drinking her coffee, taking care to pass muster as the loyal and devoted wife of the new Interim Prime Minister, no more, no less.

Dame Mona looked perfectly at ease, an authoritative figure with sharp features, short grey hair, and a pair of reading glasses suspended by a silk cord around her neck.

"In the light of the present circumstances, and the urgent need to declare a National Emergency," Dame Mona intoned, "I agree that you should take up your appointment as Interim Prime Minister until such time as Parliament can be re-established. I shall issue a directive to that effect later today."

"Thank you, Governor General," Fontaine responded, and they rose and shook hands. "May I suggest a public ceremony to install me in office? To reassure the public?"

"Certainly," Dame Mona smiled. "I look forward to meeting you again on Thursday, Senator. Shall we say at eleven am? To finalize the details."

"Thank you," Fontaine said, and they shook hands and were escorted to the door by the private secretary.

***

"I am very pleased to confirm," Dame Mona spoke into the microphone on the steps of Parliament House in Melbourne, "that today Senator The Honourable Michael Fontaine will be sworn in as Interim Prime Minister, due to the urgency of the issues that face our nation during this National Emergency."

Dame Mona paused, resting her hands at the sides of the rostrum, as deafening cheers rose from the crowd of thousands of people who crammed the intersection in front of her, and stretched away down Bourke Street. Speakers and large screens had been installed so that the public could witness this historic occasion broadcast live on TV.

Behind Dame Mona, on a specially constructed dais, sat various officials including the local and federal commissioners of police, the Chief of the Defence Force, and a swag of federal politicians who had sworn allegiance to GoodLord, refugees from the wreckage of their former parties, plus any number of business leaders and public figures who were obviously important if relatively unknown.

Sylvia sat in the front row of the bigwigs, smiling proudly through the proceedings, an aloof, commanding figure, every inch the spouse of an incoming Prime Minister.

"This swearing-in ceremony is being conducted publicly as a matter of urgency, with the TV cameras present," Dame Mona continued, "to reassure the people of Australia that their Government is in safe hands, that our glorious institutions will continue to sustain and protect us, and that all will be well in the reinvigorated Australia that we will rebuild from the ashes of the terrible fires afflicting us even as we speak."

Dame Mona paused, and smiled for the TV cameras.

"And so, with no further ado, I invite you all to witness the swearing-in ceremony conducted in the time-honoured way, with Senator the Honourable Michael Fontaine as Interim Prime Minister. The Interim Prime Minister's first task will be to appoint a National Cabinet, as decreed in the recent declaration of a National Emergency, to resolve the serious challenges our country faces."

Michael Fontaine stood and raised his hand acknowledging the cheering and clapping from the crowd. Sylvia joined him waving to the crowd after he was sworn in as Interim Prime Minister by Dame Mona Lippi, pledging to uphold the laws of the land, as loyal subjects of King William the Fifth, by the Grace of God, King of Australia and His other Realms and Territories, Head of the Commonwealth, Defender of the Faith.

***

"Your success is astounding," Freddie said to Sylvia. "It is an impressive bloodless coup. My congratulations!"

They were standing on the viewing platform of a mansion built into the hills above the Great Ocean Road, a magnificent view of Bass Strait before them. It was a brilliantly sunny day, a never-ending blue sky above them, the deep green-blue of the sea extending to the horizon.

Freddie called out a few words of Mandarin, and Fong brought a silver tray with a bottle of champagne, then left as silently as he came. Freddie opened the champagne, filled two flutes and handed one to Sylvia.

"Yes, now that Michael is Prime Minister we are half-way to our goal, in record time," she said. "The next step is the most difficult one."

"Achieving unchallenged power for Michael?" Freddie asked.

"Exactly!"

"How do you hope to do that?" Freddie looked doubtful.

"I think that we are overdue for a republic in this country. With Michael as President. In the American sense of the word."

"Wonderful! How ambitious."

"Charming as King William is," Sylvia went on, "he really is surplus to requirements. The monarchy has been redundant in this country for decades. Even more so now that Britain is too fragmented to be viable. Time to disengage."

"True enough, but quite difficult in practical terms."

"Yes, until now. Michael has the power to declare a republic in his hands. Under the national emergency laws he can do virtually anything by proclamation, with the support of the military."

"They would need to be rewarded for their support, obviously."

"As it happens," Sylvia said, "they are desperate to increase our nuclear submarine fleet, and to take a more assertive role in the security of New Guinea. And we can deliver that to them."

"Very interesting," Freddie said. "What message will you give the public?"

"Our supporters are now pretty much the majority of the country, and they'll go along with anything Michael proposes. I think that the coup de grace to the old system will be inaugurating Michael as the President of a new Republic, as the best way forward in the current crisis."

"Well said," Freddie smiled. "I can hear Michael saying that in his next speech to the nation."

"We could simply declare it as a fait accompli."

"What about the Governor General? Dame Mona Lippi?"

"How many tanks can she call into action?"

"I see that you have been reading your history. She will be replaced immediately, I presume."

"Sacked."

"I see. It all sounds high risk, but very feasible."

"So you'll back us?"

"Absolutely. I will call in favours. Especially from the military."

"Thanks, Freddie." Sylvia kissed him on the cheek, and led him inside to a large couch in a room with three hundred and sixty degree views of the beach, ocean and the hills behind them.

"Here's to the President of the Democratic Republic of Australia!" Sylvia declared, and they both raised their glasses and clinked them together.

"I'd better ring Mona Lippi and give her a heads-up," Freddie said, pulling his phone from his pocket. "We'll need her to rubber stamp the formalities."

"Will she be sympathetic?"

"There's not much she can do to oppose you."

***

Any qualms Michael Fontaine might have had about Sylvia's blockbuster proposal to shut down the Houses of Parliament and declare Australia a republic were laid to rest when, a month later, the formalities were completed. Only the Senate was retained, and the position of Governor General abolished.

Michael was inaugurated as Foundation President of the Democratic Republic of Australia at a huge Gathering at the MCG, as the new National Anthem resounded around the country from millions of TV sets, every major city crowded with GoodLord supporters demonstrating their approval of the republic.

Michael and Sylvia processed in a limousine to the steps of Parliament House, where Michael made his inauguration speech, promising a bright future for the new Democratic Republic of Australia. He declared the Houses of Parliament as the site for a new Great Assembly Hall, to be the new seat of Government for the Republic, heralding a new age of peace and prosperity.

Sylvia's high-risk strategy had paid off, not in the least tarnished by the sad news of Dame Mona Lippi's death a few days after Michael's inauguration.

Apparently Dame Mona had killed herself. Sylvia made sure that the news media declared Dame Mona's death the result of deep depression after a family tragedy in the recent fires. The full details of the story could not be verified due to the guidelines applied to all the reporting about the National Emergency.

Homage was due to the Fontaine Government for this "wonderful leap into the future," as the newspapers put it, praising President Fontaine's "sterling leadership and inspiring speeches."

This line of thinking was echoed by Zelda Freestone in one of her various statements to the press, calling Michael "a new leader for a new age," which in her view included "a return to common sense, free enterprise and the abolition of bureaucracy and red tape."

Sylvia laughed at Zelda's constant references for the need to abolish red tape, given her backing for the bureaucratic enforcement of limits to freedom of movement across the country. Nonetheless, the vociferous support of everyone who mattered was vital to the success of the Fontaine Government, and Sylvia rang Zelda to thank her for her comments.

Michael's rise to power was built on the back of catastrophic disasters. He had risen to the occasion, with a deft ability to reassure and comfort people with just the right words, making them feel safe in a threatening world.

With Sylvia backing him, Michael's political career had become a yellow brick road of golden opportunities, for as many years as they wished to rule the country.

***

No one was more impressed or more supportive of Michael's rise to power than Sylvia's father. Victor Rojo was Sylvia's biggest fan, telling her how proud he was of her rise to such dizzy heights.

"The First Lady of Australia, no less," he said when he heard the news, beaming with pride.

Whenever Sylvia felt the need for peace and quiet, Alex would chauffeur her in her favourite black SUV to visit Victor for a couple of hours, chatting on the balcony of his mansion in a gated community built on a former golf course in Beaumaris, a pleasant bayside suburb.

Victor Rojo had managed well since Eileen's death. He pottered about the garden, greeting Sylvia in his gardening clothes, enthusing about his hydrangeas and the greenhouse he had installed in his vast backyard. Every morning he walked along the beach with a dog he rescued from the pound, a black and white bitzer called Ned, after the famous bushranger. To all intents and purposes, Victor seemed quite content.

Since passing over nominal management of his supermarkets to Jack, while making sure that both Sylvia and Naomi were well looked after, Victor had more time on his hands, he said, than he knew what to do with. What this seemed to mean was that he was no longer spending eighteen hours a day hard at work.

In reality, control of his supermarkets remained in Victor's hands, and Jack chafed at the constraints of "having to please Father all the time." In Sylvia's view, Victor's continued involvement was all that prevented Jack from driving them bankrupt.

On her way back from one of these visits, Alex paid a lot of attention to his rear view mirror, finally saying to Sylvia, "Ma'am, I'm pretty certain we're being followed. There's a car behind us that I noticed on the way over to your father's house."

"What sort of people do they look like, Alex?" Sylvia said.

"A middle aged couple, driving a stock standard Toyota, but they know the tricks of the trade."

"Has this happened before, Alex?"

"I've seen them before, but I wasn't sure if it was just coincidence. This time I'm certain. There'll be another car or two involved, replacing each other at regular intervals."

"I see. Have you noticed anyone following you when you've been driving Michael?"

"No, Ma'am."

"OK. I'll have to make enquiries about this," Sylvia said. "Keep an eye on them, and see if they turn up next time we go out. Maybe we'll take a special trip, check them out."

"Yes, ma'am," Alex said. "Good idea. One possibility is to take them on a wild goose chase, and arrange for someone to join us later in a separate car, and then track them down. Actually a team of two or three cars to assist us would be ideal."

"An excellent idea," Sylvia said. "Oh, and Alex, we'll keep this between you and me."

"Understood, Ma'am."

Being under surveillance was a troubling thought. Sylvia wondered how long this had been going on, but of course Alex was good at spotting that sort of thing, so maybe it was recent. She didn't use a limousine like Michael, but had Alex drive her Honda so she could work on her laptop in the back seat. Maybe she would need to swap cars more often.

It seemed likely that Sam Newbold's death had aroused suspicions with the police, or more likely the security agencies. Or it may simply be an outcome of looking at who would benefit most from Sam's death, which made Michael's victory in the Senate election an obvious choice.

It also was troubling to think of her visits to Freddie Wu being reported back to the huge security apparatus that had accumulated in Australia over the decades. The established security forces would have to be dismantled, but that would take time, no matter how much effort Noah put into replacing them. Best to make her own arrangements.

***

Later that day Sylvia rang Freddie Wu on her burner phone, to avoid being followed to a meeting with him. She asked Freddie for a security team of three cars to follow her car. She would get Alex to drive her around Melbourne on a pre-arranged route, allowing Freddie's security people to observe who was following them, and then sort things out.

"Can you fix this for me?" Sylvia asked Freddie on the phone.

"We can certainly give them something to think about. Fong has excellent contacts in the local criminal communities, with all the necessary skills. Your phones will be tapped and traced, of course, then there may be break-ins to check your laptop etc. And they will investigate everyone you know."

"Yes, I understand that. We have excellent security at GoodLord. Everything going in and out is scanned. We also have CCTV and a 24-hour security presence. The same is the case at home."

"Good. Just make your little trip, and then after Fong's team intervenes, Alex will take you straight home. He will know what to do."

"Thanks, Freddie."

There was no point telling Michael anything about this situation. He would just worry pointlessly, and do nothing to change his careless approach to security. It would be better to tighten up security around him without saying anything. In any event, it seemed more likely that she herself was the person of interest to these security people, whoever they were, on account of Sam Newbold's death, no doubt because he was a big wig politician. She would need to keep her head down for some time without making it obvious, and come up with a longer term solution.

***

A few days later, Alex drove Sylvia around town, finally heading for Chadstone Shopping Centre.

"They're behind us again," Alex said. "Different car this time, a grey Nissan. They'll get a surprise once we get inside the shopping centre car park."

They drove slowly towards the entrance of the massive shopping centre open air car park, Alex constantly checking his rear view mirror, and listening to his earpiece.

"Any moment now," he said.

They slowly crossed a mini roundabout, as a silver BMW swung across the front of them, accelerating away, then crashing into a car entering the roundabout behind them.

"Nice," Alex said.

Sylvia glanced into the side mirror and saw a well-dressed blonde get out of the BMW and harangue the driver of the car she hit.

Alex chuckled. "That'll keep them busy," he said. "Her passenger will be taking photos, maybe we'll find out more about who's been following us."

Cars started honking their horns as the BMW driver kept arguing with the occupants of the grey Nissan that had been following them. The two of them were blocking traffic now, backing up to the previous roundabout in the mini highway system surrounding the shopping centre.

Alex drove on, exiting on the other side of Chadstone.

"Our security team is still following us, checking on whether there's a backup surveillance car still on our tail," he said.

"Thanks, Alex," Sylvia said.

This intervention was only a temporary measure, Freddie had told her, but they had to find out who they were. As it was, Sylvia had limited her meetings with Freddie, at least until they knew a little more about the people spying on her.

CHAPTER 12

HARRY

Rita and I sit in our lounge room watching news reports on TV of the massive fires enveloping Canberra, appalled and frightened. People attempting to escape any way they can, abandoning their cars on the roads, trying to catch buses and train services that quit working due to the fires, with disastrous results.

"Who would have thought it would come to this?" Rita says softly, tears running down her cheeks. "Why can't the Government do something?"

"They're too focused on petty squabbling," I say. "They can't even run a chook raffle in normal times."

What can you say in the face of a tragedy on this scale? Canberra is over six hundred kilometres away, but it might as well be next door. It's immediate, and catastrophic.

We don't get much sleep that night, talking about what has happened in Canberra, and if the same sort of thing would happen to Melbourne.

The news media relay the endless human tragedies, interviewing distraught people who have lost their houses, grieving parents and so on, to the point where it becomes too hard to take. No one seems to have any overview on what is happening.

In the midst of this catastrophe, it's clear that the Hanson Government has comprehensively failed. Michael Fontaine calls a major rally in Melbourne, and somehow talks the Governor General, Dame Mona Lippi, into declaring him Interim Prime Minister.

On TV, Fontaine towers over Dame Mona Lippi, a stern, purposeful little figure, clutching a Bible and looking up at Fontaine like a pygmy appraising an elephant, as she swears him in to replace Barney Hanson. I struggle to catch a glimpse of her face close up, to check whether the scar from the stone thrown through Bluestone Corporation's window has left any long term traces on her forehead, but the view is too distant.

It's a brilliant move by Fontaine, you have to give it to him. And he certainly has public support, as well as backing from everyone who matters in the country, from the military, billionaires and the news media, to all the powers-that-be at every level of government and business.

Who knows what might happen next? But the general feeling is that now at least we have a Prime Minister who looks and sounds like a leader, and warrants our trust.

Rita is sceptical, though. "How do we know that Michael Fontaine can fix this crisis," she says. "He's had no experience in Government. This isn't just about making speeches and praying for divine assistance."

Good old practical Rita. She has a point. Although you have to say that anybody will be better than Barney Hanson as PM, not to mention the vast majority of the other fools in Parliament, who all appear to regard themselves as leaders, without a shred of evidence to support their delusions of grandeur. All in all, I think that we are probably better off with GoodLord running the country, but I don't say that to Rita.

Fontaine's subsequent move to the republic and the Presidency is a stroke of genius, whatever anyone might say about the threat to democracy. There is no point messing about when the whole country is under threat.

***

I keep the cash donations in the sturdy safe installed in my office, inside a large cabinet normally providing shelving for stationery. This is where I hide donations while they are in transit. It's the old-fashioned type of safe, with a large steel wheel that you spin around, a left-right-left dial, and a strong key lock. It's very heavy, bolted to the floor, and about waist height with enough room to hold a substantial amount of cash.

The metal stationery cabinet has a healthy lock in it too. No one ever comes into my office except people I invite for meetings or a chat, and the cleaners. No one knows the safe is there, only me and Noah Kowalski.

Much as I'm shocked by Neil Bautervich's revelation about Noah switching sides and secretly helping GoodLord, I'm reconciling to it now. Politics is politics. So when Noah rings to make his move, I'm ready for it.

"I'll come over at lunchtime," Noah says on the phone that morning. "We'll need to clean the safe out."

"Why?" I ask.

"Talk to you soon," Noah says.

It strikes me immediately that Noah is going to do a runner, taking the cash with him. I wonder whether he will ask me to go with him.

It turns out that Noah is ready to move to the GoodLord offices right away. He's taken home all the files he can carry over the preceding week or two, and everything else he needs is in the laptop in the bag he is carrying on his shoulder. He looks calm and decisive, not at all like a rat leaving a sinking ship, and says that he has booked leave to cover his getaway. No one in his office knows that he has permanently gone.

Basically he's defecting to GoodLord in the grand political tradition of going over to the opposition when the future looks more promising on the other side of the fence. It's also clear that he expects me to go with him.

Noah has left his BMW in the official Party car park, with the keys left in his desk. There was no way he could announce his departure publicly in his former workplace, he would have been lucky to get out of there alive. So here we are, sneaking off to the enemy camp, me as Noah's consultant at GoodLord, apparently, on a semi-official basis, without even a cursory wave goodbye to our long years with the Labour Party.

I have nothing I need to take with me, except like Noah, my laptop. We stash them in the boot of my car together with a couple of large bags full of cash, and I drive him to the bayside premises of GoodLord Inc, like bank robbers making a getaway with the loot. We ignore the smoke haze on the horizon; life goes on so long as the brunt of disasters falls on someone else.

Noah explains that there are offices waiting for us at GoodLord. His office is part of the executive suite, mine is located in their admin section, suitably anonymous and easily accessible from the street. My consultancy-style deal is to continue, he tells me, it's simply a matter of changing a few minor details on my business card. Come and go as I please, no questions asked, and report directly to him.

"It's my old job in a different location for me too," he explains on the way there. "Except with double the money the Party paid me and a central role in the future of GoodLord Inc."

God knows the detail of what Noah's deal with GoodLord involves, but as we drive up to the luxurious office block housing the GoodLord bayside offices, I can see that it's going to be top drawer.

We're greeted in the foyer by a young woman in her thirties, introduced to me by Noah as Anna Kalajian, Vice President Public Affairs. She certainly looks the part, brisk and elegant, jet black hair, golden brown complexion and a smart business suit.

"Welcome to GoodLord," she says, and it's obvious that they know each other. "Sylvia is waiting for you in her office," she adds.

For all Noah's usual brash behaviour and rat cunning, he seems to be a man on a mission, more serious than I can remember in a long time. After all, he has a lot riding on this shift. It's a major defection, but of course it's happening all around us, just that he is a bigger catch than most.

I walk behind Anna and Noah as they chat casually to each other, and we arrive on the top floor in a large mirrored elevator. As we step out, Sylvia Fontaine, familiar from my TV screen, stands there, all smiles and bonhomie.

She is tall and imperious, fortyish, her long black hair severely pulled back from a striking face. A prominent nose, dark complexion, and keen intelligent eyes.

"Noah," Sylvia Fontaine says. "Welcome. Good to see you here at last. Where you belong."

Noah chuckles. Again, the two of them seem familiar.

"This is Harry Mott, an indispensable member of my team," he introduces me. "Harry, this is Sylvia Fontaine, CEO of GoodLord."

"Good to meet you, Harry," Sylvia says.

It's like being introduced to royalty. I feel drawn to her immediately, there is such an aura about her. Michael Fontaine is not alone with his charisma, his wife has her fair share as well.

We all troop into her office, a huge lavish affair with a view across a park to the bay. There are framed photos on the wall of her and Michael Fontaine meeting with all sorts of dignitaries, and it's easy to see what a vital part of the power couple she is.

We sit in large leather armchairs, and Sylvia explains that Michael is in Sydney, but will fly back that afternoon. And then she chats amiably about how Michael Fontaine and GoodLord will turn Australia around in the face of its worst crisis since the Second World War.

Sitting there listening to her, I believe every word she says. Even before I meet Michael Fontaine face to face, I'm a convert to GoodLord.

***

"Welcome aboard, Harry," Michael Fontaine says when I'm called to his office to meet him after lunch. He's sitting at a massive desk, his desktop computer open at his Facebook page, and his office walls are covered with photos of meetings with the rich and famous. A set of golf clubs is set in a corner, and I notice a couple of golfing trophies on a cadenza.

We are on the topmost floor of his GoodLord offices in Brighton, with a view of the Bay even grander than the one from his wife's office. However, the new President and his wife will soon be moving to Raheen, a heritage mansion on the Yarra River just outside the Central Business District, but apparently they'll keep these premises as the GoodLord HQ. How they will distinguish between the business of GoodLord Inc and Government business should be an interesting issue.

"Sorry I couldn't catch up with you earlier," he adds as he stands up to shake my hand. "I've spent a couple of days in Sydney. Dreadful floods there, good to be back."

"I'm pleased to meet you. You're the most famous person I've ever met, Mr President," I say. He's an impressive man close up, large, genial, with wavy blonde hair going silver, and an engaging smile with film star teeth.

Fontaine laughs. "I hope you're not disappointed?" And he waves me to one of the armchairs placed in front of his desk.

"Not at all. Even better than on TV," I say.

He shines a brilliant smile on me, says "Call me Michael," and I grin back like a young fan meeting a rock star. I don't have to lie. I like what I see. Compared to the average politician, the sort of people too important to talk to you whenever you come across them, well, Fontaine looks pretty good.

"Settling in OK?" Fontaine asks.

"Certainly," I say. "A great work environment you've got here."

"Excellent!" Fontaine says. And we chat for a while about the footy. I tell him that I barrack for Carlton footy club, and he happens to be a Richmond fan. We speculate on how long it would take to get Richmond back in shape after not winning a Grand Final for so long, and he tells me that GoodLord is addressing the challenge of maintaining sport and recreation for survivors of the National Disaster.

"I've been thinking of giving the club a helping hand," Fontaine says. "Perhaps even buying it and giving them a financial shot in the arm. What do you think, Harry?"

"Good idea," I say. "Maybe you could buy the whole league? Every club, give them a new start without all the bureaucracy? And maybe abolish umpires?"

"I can see that you're a rascal, Harry," Fontaine laughs. "GoodLord needs people like you. People with initiative. Give me a call if you need anything."

Imagine meeting the President in your workplace, having a yarn and a laugh, and then popping back to your office to do whatever the hell you want.

I'm impressed, and increasingly feel I have done the right thing following Noah to GoodLord.

***

I've barely sat down at my desk before Sylvia Fontaine knocks on the door and strides in, waving her hand for me to sit as I start to rise to my feet.

"Thought I'd see how you're settling in," she says, sitting down in the one spare chair in my office. She smiles across my desk at me, and I wonder what she wants.

"Off to a good start," I say. "I'm just back from a chat with the President."

"You can call him Michael," she says, laughing. "I've just been talking to Noah. You've known him for a long time, I gather?"

"Over twenty years now," I say.

"Good friends, I imagine?" Sylvia asks.

"I think you could say that it's a comfortable work relationship," I reply. "We both like to keep work separate from home."

"I see," she says. "A very competent person, Noah."

"One of the best in his field, no doubt about it," I say, trying to sound more enthusiastic than I feel. *Where the hell is this going?*

"And Sam Newbold? Did you know him well? A tragic case, that awful business."

"Yes, it was terrible. But, no, I never worked with Sam Newbold. He was in a different Labour faction to Noah, pretty much opponents, in fact. But I knew him by reputation, of course. An outstanding leader. One of the best public speakers I know of."

"Yes, I used to watch him on TV. A great loss to Labour. Not that it matters any more, of course. Their time has passed."

"Absolutely," I say, wondering what Sylvia Fontaine really thinks about Sam Newbold's death. *A gift from the gods, I would have thought, giving her husband an easy passage to the Senate, at first, and now, unbelievably, the move to President. Serendipity doesn't come into it. More like a bloody miracle.*

"I must be off," Sylvia says. "Nice chatting to you, Harry. Please let me know any time there's anything I can help you with."

"Thank you," I say, trying to imagine any circumstances where I would ask for her help, a lowly shit-kicker at the Queen's court. Perhaps I should bow, or go down on one knee.

Sylvia smiles, rises from her chair looking immaculate in a well-cut pantsuit and understated but very expensive jewellry. She walks off briskly down the corridor, head held high, looking neither right nor left, her regal progress leaving the office staff she passes by flustered and whispering together.

After that visit to my office, the people in adjoining offices and in the open plan area are obviously more curious about me. I'm clearly someone with connections to the top, and I receive a few more hellos and attempts at conversation at the coffee machine, all unwanted.

I tell Noah about Sylvia's visit, and her questions.

"What's that all about?" I ask him. "She asked me if I knew Sam Newbold."

"She's no fool. She's fucking lethal. Just make sure you never cross her. Probably wondering about people's allegiances with so many new staff, most of them on the make."

"Including us?" I say.

"Yeah, including us," Noah grins, lighting a new cigarette from the stub of his current one.

"It's a new ball game here, all right. No need to scrabble for funds from Chinese donors. Obviously they're deeply embedded in GoodLord already."

"Well, they're deeply embedded everywhere, aren't they," Noah says. "Like all the other millionaires. Part of the political landscape."

"Yeah. Could be a problem, that, don't you reckon?" I say.

"How do you mean?"

"Chinese influence, as they call it."

"Well, there's always fucking influence, right? Millionaires, lobby groups, all sorts of nut cases, you name it. Just follow the money, it has to come from somewhere."

"Yeah, guess you're right," I say.

He's looking surly, so I let it go. I wonder if Noah has ever been a youthful idealist, full of high-minded opinions about the need to help the poor, etcetera, but despite his working class roots and career in Labour politics I've never heard a glimmer of idealism or ideology from him. Strictly a numbers man, he might have had a great career on the money markets.

I can imagine him as a foul-mouthed investment banker, killing off the opposition as he gambles billions of dollars of other people's money on complex deals that result in the destruction of the environment of vulnerable third world countries, while simultaneously bankrupting suburban mums and dads who put their nest egg into his infallible investment vehicles.

***

My move to GoodLord provokes a blizzard of angry emails and text messages from people in the Labour Party I barely know. God knows what sort of onslaught Noah is enduring, but like me he couldn't care less.

Ben Reilly's approach is more personal. "What the hell do you think you're doing?" he demands at my front door one night, loud and distraught like an outraged husband searching for his wandering wife.

"What do you mean?" I say, and invite him indoors. It's raining heavily, and he appears to be soaked, as though he has walked all the way from his house to mine to say his piece without a raincoat or an umbrella. Fortunately Rita is out having coffee with a girlfriend, which makes this confrontation Ben insists on having somewhat easier.

He must have been stewing over my defection to GoodLord to the point where he couldn't stop himself turning up on my doorstep and putting me straight.

"Don't what-do-you-mean me, for Christ's sake," he yells once we reach the lounge room. "You're up to your neck in this insane betrayal with Noah Kowalski, which you must have been planning for fucking ages. Just give me the facts. Why did you piss off to GoodLord?"

"Not too many facts in this game," I say. "Noah asked me to join him when he left, and I said yes, and drove him over to GoodLord and signed on with him. End of story."

"Bullshit," Ben says, all red-faced and glaring. "How the fuck could you betray the Party on a whim?"

"Not a whim, and not a betrayal," I say. "It's a change of job. Yes, so far as Noah is concerned, you can compare him to a retiring Party leader joining the big banks or a mining company. But so what? It happens. In my case, I'm still a consultant to a political party. Just a different one."

"It happens, it happens," Ben moans, beside himself. "Still a consultant. Fuck you!" he shouts, and he storms off home into the rain without another word.

I suppose my "defection" with Noah to GoodLord is yet another nail in the coffin of Ben's beloved Labour Party. Of course, he doesn't know the half of it. For all these years Ben has had no knowledge of my informant relationship with Neil Bautervich, nor my tangled involvement in the politics around Sam Newbold, let alone the fact that I witnessed his ugly death. I feel relieved that Ben is still ignorant of the whole story, as well as sad that it has come to this. It seems unavoidable, though, a disaster that has been waiting to happen.

Of course, it's even tougher where Rita is concerned. In fact, Rita is so stunned by my move to GoodLord that she seems paralyzed. She doesn't argue with me, or try to convince me of a massive error of judgement. Her silence expresses her utter disgust, as though I've been caught mugging a little old lady, or thrashing a cute little puppy dog to death.

For Rita, what I did is simply immoral. Her deeply committed Labour family is also shocked. I am the betrayer of the new faith in Labour politics that they clung to when their old faith in the Church ran out of juice. I should have seen this coming, but it just never occurred to me. People don't seem to understand that politics is essentially meaningless.

My own view is pragmatic. The old politics is no longer viable. The Labour Party has been taken over by private school boys who want to be PM no matter what it takes, even if it means joining the Labour Party, while the Coalition is a pale shadow of the original benign autocracy that Sir Robert Menzies created back in the 1950s, a welding together of wealthy graziers and big city lawyers. Welcome to the new politics. However, I don't think I could have shocked everyone more than if I had announced my conversion to a neo-Nazi party. Despite their cloak of free thinking and tolerance, I am now beyond the pale, an insidious foreign intruder who has finally revealed his true colours.

Rita's shocked silence persists day and night, and leaves me sleeping in the spare room, formerly Jesse's bedroom. His rock star posters are still on the wall, plus some of his clothes in the wardrobe. Thankfully Jesse is working in Sydney, pursuing his career in IT, so there's one less source of disapproval in the immediate vicinity. But as the news spreads amongst our friends, our social life collapses like a pricked balloon. Much like my marriage.

One downside of living in the same neighbourhood and having the same job all your adult life is that when a crisis hits, a cat's cradle of social relationships unravels.

Whereas we used to have regular meals together with Ben and Fiona in either of our houses, only a couple of kilometres apart, or go to the pub or on some outing, that all ends more or less overnight. One thing is for sure, we won't be spending Christmas at their beach house this year.

Rita and Fiona keep on with their catch ups, going to yoga together, meeting for coffee. I can tell that they are flailing about hoping to find a solution. Ben and I have not spoken since his outburst when he came to visit me in the rain. It looks like the dead weight of unspoken secrets over so many years has sunk us.

***

The only close friend who takes all the hoo-ha about my change of allegiances with a grain of salt is Anton Nakamura. He has long since lost all interest in politics, and treats the political scene as nothing but an obscene joke.

"You're taking a hell of a risk by moving to GoodLord," he murmurs one afternoon over green tea in his lounge room.

I'm gazing at a print on the wall behind his head, a blue ship sailing in a vibrant red sea, the only anomaly in a perfectly conventional house, nothing out of place, expensively renovated. Out the window, in the backyard, stands Anton's greenhouse full of orchids that have won awards at garden shows. Orchid shows? I'm not sure. His bookshelves are lined with books on Renaissance architecture and art. The house reflects the man.

"What do you mean?" I ask.

"Your whole life has been tied up with the so-called Labour Party," he says. "Yes, I know," he adds as I try to interrupt, "you're neutral, just a consultant. But it's never looked that way to anybody else. And now you've spat in their faces. Noah Kowalski is obviously a politician who would sell his own mother to get into power. So no one is surprised when he jumps ship. But you're not. It looks like you don't love them any more. They'll never take you back."

"I have never loved them. And I don't want to go back. But never mind that. What do I do about Rita?"

"God knows," Anton laughs.

"Well, thanks a bloody lot!"

"Self inflicted pain, the worst sort," he grimaces. "Your only options appear to be either to resign and work in something else, or retire. Then Rita might forgive you."

Anton is sitting in the same lounge room he has lived in since university. The house was worth bugger-all back then, but is now worth a fortune in a crazy inner-city real estate market that is throwing big bucks at disused dog kennels. Fortunately it's on high ground, above the flooding from the Maribyrnong River, now a frequent feature of life in this part of Melbourne.

Walter Silum, Anton's partner, has kindly gone out for the afternoon after I fetched up at their front door looking woebegone. They are living the good life in retirement. Anton has racked up a small fortune in superannuation, ironically for a guy who started off so poor, and has saved his way to a life of ease. Nice holidays, splendid meals in expensive restaurants, and a new Audi in the garage. I can't complain, myself, but I do envy the fact that he inherited a house. Growing up poor is something you can still feel as you age. People you know inherit stuff, and you don't. But at least I haven't had to endure anything like Anton's experience of prejudice against gays, not to mention being asked where the name "Nakamura" comes from and being labelled a "Jap".

For all the risks that Anton has taken, openly flouting the anti-gay laws of bygone years, now enjoying his freedom under the new laws for gay marriage, his life as a conscientious accountant in a dull job seems to make sense compared to my erratic record of working on the margins. To the point where it currently threatens the one thing I really believe in, my marriage to Rita.

Anton has always been the only person I talk to about Rita, I feel embarrassed with anyone else. He has known the both of us since we first met, and he has been good friends with Rita since schooldays. I always trust his judgement, impartial and honest.

Now, though, it's clear that he thinks I'm a damn fool to defect to GoodLord, and that Rita doesn't deserve that sort of idiocy.

I trail home, and endure another silent meal with Rita, wondering if it might be better to simply retire from work, since I lack the courage to jump off a high building, and a slow death by ostracism holds no attraction for me either.

PART FOUR

UNFINISHED BUSINESS

CHAPTER 13

SYLVIA

It was obvious once Noah Kowalski arrived at GoodLord that he was a definite asset to the new Fontaine Government. He had an astute grip on the key political issues, making a competent start on his new portfolio of National Security and Home Affairs, as well as an impressive contribution to the security meetings that Sylvia chaired at GoodLord.

He was backed up by his offsider Harry Mott, a thickset man in his early fifties, with a bald head and dark suit, shirt and tie, who looked like some union thug and came and went as he pleased, doing who knows what.

"Now we've got Noah's offsider with us, Harry Mott, we need to include him in the surveillance reports," Sylvia said to Anna Kalajian over coffee soon after Harry's arrival.

"No problem," Anna said. "Harry is already bobbing up in the reports because of his close links to Noah."

"OK, then. Extend the surveillance to include Harry full time. Give me a preliminary report on his background, contacts, family and so on by next week."

Sylvia thought about discussing her own problem of being under surveillance, but decided against it. Freddie had told her that she was definitely under surveillance by one of the Australian security agencies, although he couldn't be certain which one, and had been emphatic that she should not tell anyone.

"In these situations you take logic to its ultimate conclusion," Freddie said. "So many people tell their secrets to their best friend or their partner, and then are surprised when everybody knows their business. Telling no one should be observed to the letter. And certainly do not tell Noah or anyone in GoodLord security."

Sylvia would never tell someone like Noah Kowalski under any circumstances anyway, since this would reveal a weakness. And then she still had to consider the possibility that Noah had her under surveillance as well.

Anna's initial surveillance report on Harry Mott was innocuous enough, although given that he was involved in an extensive political donations racket, like Noah, you would assume that other temptations had fallen his way. But apparently Harry had not submitted to them, so far at least.

***

In one of his early meetings with the inner sanctum running the Fontaine Government, Noah proposed the construction of Protection Barriers on the outskirts of the major cities.

"We can already see the pressure building up. Refugees in regional areas are streaming into the cities, overwhelming essential services, and in some cases presenting a serious security risk," Noah said, looking around the table at Michael and Sylvia, with Anna Kalajian, Charlotte Hung and Harry Mott making up the numbers.

Sylvia could see immediately that Noah had hit the nail on the head. The only way of preventing the rise of homelessness and the breakdown of law and order in the main population centres, possibly leading to unrest and terrorism that was too close for comfort, was to build physical barriers.

"That sounds like an excellent idea," she said immediately, repressing the urge to counter Noah's argument. Sylvia sat back and smiled, pleasantly suggesting that Noah submit a detailed proposal to their next meeting. Better for Noah to own the concept, and run with it, and then find other ways to counter his influence. She would have to rely on Charlotte Hung to keep Noah's financial dealings in line.

Sylvia could see that Charlotte was cool and calm in her dealings with Noah, politely pointing out any dubious aspects of any contracts he proposed.

"Noah is a very good negotiator, but he takes on too much risk," Charlotte told Sylvia.

"Yes, he's a gambler at heart," Sylvia said.

"Does he get into serious debt?"

"The rumour is that he owes a lot of money," Sylvia smiled. "But I think that is the only reckless thing about him. He's a very clever politician."

"Yes, I understand," Charlotte said.

Who knew what Charlotte's attitude to politics was, but two things were certain. She would have learned a great deal from "Uncle" Freddie about handling people like Noah Kowalski, and she would be across every detail of Noah's profile, even without access to the surveillance that Anna Kalajian was conducting on Sylvia's behalf.

***

Closer to home, Sylvia was deeply involved in planning the demolition of the Houses of Parliament in Melbourne to make way for a brand new Great Assembly Hall, a monumental building for the new GoodLord power elite to meet for Gatherings and to debate the issues of the day. In the meantime, Michael conducted

Government business from his spacious office on the ground floor of Raheen, a heritage mansion overlooking the Yarra, just outside the business district, and now the Presidential Residence with security guards patrolling the perimeter.

Raheen had everything Sylvia could imagine, from a massive master bedroom to a study with a small library, an indoor swimming pool, extensive gardens, tennis courts, a large ballroom, conference room, and a dining room that could seat fifty guests.

Sylvia decided that Presidential Dinners, held at Raheen, would be a useful way to entertain people of influence. She invited long-term supporters from the business world like Zelda Freestone and Marcus Gore, as well as the top military brass and police officials, and a range of politicians and bureaucrats.

Charlotte Hung and husband George were regular guests too, of course, but Freddie Wu declined Sylvia's invitation.

"Inevitably there will be moments when our nations' interests will not align perfectly," Freddie said, "and it is best to remain at a respectable distance, publicly at least."

Sylvia understood this to mean that on occasion Freddie would deliver demands from Shanghai that may not be palatable to the Fontaine Government, and the resulting fuss would not be worth the trouble. An early example was China's "request" for more access for their navy to Australian ports, not a popular move in the current state of chaos across the nation, but something the Government had to accede to.

Similarly, Freddie took to addressing Michael as "Mr President," at least on first encounter, and always when in front of other people outside their inner circle. Now that the Fontaine Government was in full control of the country, Freddie appeared to have decided to move to the sidelines, at least in a public sense.

Even without Freddie's presence to liven things up, the dinners provided Sylvia with the opportunity of reinforcing her role as First Lady, hosting these brilliant occasions with regal authority, networking with her allies, and withholding invitations from anyone who showed even a glimmer of disloyalty.

Whatever their background, members of the GoodLord elite were impressed by meeting with Sylvia in the glamorous surroundings of Raheen, complete with chandeliers, exquisite artwork, and a legion of servants.

The one exception to the unstinted admiration of Sylvia's Presidential dinners by GoodLord's wealthy supporters was Zelda Freestone.

Zelda in old age had become a caricature of a fabulously wealthy billionaire, festooned with large ugly pieces of expensive jewellry, her pudgy figure shoehorned into designer dresses as she pronounced workers' demands for fair pay to be greedy and unreasonable. "Workers in other countries are happy to work for a dollar a day," she added during one of her press conferences, to Sylvia's mind another example of the need for GovMedia to control the narrative, since these sorts of comments, true or not, were pointless and inflammatory.

Now, it seemed, Zelda saw herself as the Fontaine Government's major patron. She seemed to believe that her support, as the richest individual in the country with a vice-like grip on key resources like iron ore, was the only reason for Michael's elevation as President.

This meant that Zelda's direct access to Michael became a right that she took advantage of whenever she felt like it, and she seemed able to bully him into agreeing on the spot with any feral demand she cared to put forward, leaving Sylvia to put the pieces back together again.

In general, Zelda behaved as though she had no idea of the extent of Sylvia's influence, or the power of players in the background, like Freddie Wu and his influential friends. Even Marcus Gore, who owned every major newspaper in the country and had been known to manipulate a change of government back in the day, was unable to dent Zelda's enormous ego, despite publishing a variety of articles dripping in sarcasm about everything from her bad taste in clothes to her deluded sense of her own importance.

"She's just a dim-witted heiress pissing away her father's fortune," Marcus was reported as growling at one of his editors, a comment that apparently ricocheted around the big end of town without even grazing Zelda Freestone.

It was an awkward situation, given that the Fontaine Government relied on the vast mineral wealth mined by Zelda's companies to prop up the economy badly damaged by endless natural disasters.

Zelda's mission to cut Government "waste," meaning the entire public service budget and all forms of taxation, accelerated. She kept on demanding these absolute "freedoms" despite the carnage experienced in every corner of the economy except, of course, the export of minerals to China.

There were grumbles, too, about Zelda's virtual monopoly in the iron ore market, with rumours of deals that locked out any competition.

Unlike Zelda, whatever their demands, at least Freddie Wu's billionaire friends kept their political views to themselves. What was needed from Zelda was a better sense of what the public needed to hear and less grandstanding, but Sylvia knew that it was a stretch to imagine her ever becoming an advocate of civic harmony.

The GoodLord mantra was that every life was precious in the eyes of the Lord, a sentiment that was in tune with the old Aussie dictum of a fair go for one and all, no matter who you were. A myth that had to be sustained in the name of public order. There had to be a way around Zelda, and Sylvia decided on a carrot-and-stick approach.

"We need to give Zelda something, Michael. Some sort of honour or award. It's important that we get on the front foot with her as soon as possible. Keep her inside the tent."

"Yes, I think you're right," Michael said. "But what do you give to someone who already has everything?"

"Something that only Governments can give. Honours, diplomatic appointments, that kind of thing."

"Ah, yes," Michael said with a sigh. Sylvia could see that just thinking about the Zelda issue was painful for him.

"How about producing a new honours list, with her at the top. We need to replace all the old stuff, anyway. We could call it the President's Medal. And Zelda could be the first recipient."

Michael readily agreed, and Sylvia instructed Anna Kalajian to issue a public statement making the first award to Zelda Freestone for exceptional service to the Democratic Republic of Australia. Sylvia then went ahead with plans for the conferring of the President's Medal on Zelda at the next President's Dinner.

The evening was the biggest and best yet. Zelda was in her element, wearing a flowing evening gown of red silk, with a grotesquely huge diamond necklace glittering at her throat.

Michael Fontaine did the honours, handing over the medal, made of finely wrought silver according to Sylvia's design, picturing a kangaroo at rest in the middle of a map of Australia.

"Never has an award for excellence been better deserved," Michael intoned in his brief speech, "to the leading light of the mining industry, and indeed the premier businessperson in this fine country of ours."

After Zelda's thank-you speech, a rambling justification for digging enormous holes absolutely anywhere that minerals of any value at all might be found, Sylvia ended the presentation with an invitation to Zelda to represent Australia at the upcoming Global Rare Earths Conference, a meeting of the leading mining countries to be held in Singapore the following month.

Zelda looked suitably impressed, and the rest of the evening was dominated by her pronouncements about rare earth minerals at her side of the huge circular dining table, designed to put to rest any dissatisfaction with the seating arrangements. This had the disadvantage of placing everyone within earshot of someone as loud as Zelda.

Sylvia suffered in silence, leaving Zelda's opinionated statements to fly past her head unchallenged. She knew for a cold fact, from reliable sources, that Zelda often referred to her as "that stuck-up wog" to their mutual acquaintances, and in general made no secret of her contempt for Sylvia as someone who owed her position to her husband. Given that Zelda had inherited her huge fortune from her father, Sylvia wondered why she viewed herself as some sort of self-made success, but she was content to bide her time before evening up the score.

The Zelda problem was exacerbated by developments in New Guinea. Aside from the ongoing issue of China's dominance of the Pacific and Indian oceans, a new fly in the ointment was the escalation of tensions on the New Guinea border.

This was yet another opportunity for Zelda to loudly complain that the Fontaine Government should do more to protect Australian mining interests close to the Papua New Guinea border with Irian Jaya.

"More Australian boots on the ground are badly needed in New Guinea," Zelda proclaimed, suddenly an expert on foreign policy and military strategy.

Sylvia was appalled by the way the New Guinea problem had been allowed to fester by previous Governments, leading to Australian troops patrolling the border with the New Guinea forces without sufficient backup. Predictably enough Michael vacillated on the best course of action, while Noah Kowalski urged him to follow the advice of the Australian military to send in more troops.

Freddie Wu, of course, counselled that quiet diplomacy was the best option, and offered his assistance. However, the dithering about that ensued across the relevant Government departments soon meant that Javanese troops were able to flood into the border areas in pursuit of indigenous rebels, driving back the small number of Australian soldiers to the coast with heavy losses. Reinforcements arrived too late and were only able to rescue the survivors of the forced march in retreat. Effectively this meant the loss of Papua New Guinea as an ally to Australia, as the PNG Government appointed a new Prime Minister who immediately agreed to the Javanese demands.

"What happened?" Sylvia demanded of Michael.

"I have no idea," Michael said wearily. "Noah slipped the leash, the military applied pressure to take a more aggressive approach, Foreign Affairs couldn't decide what to do, and the Javanese beat us to the punch."

"The whole thing could have been avoided with the right diplomatic moves," Sylvia said. "Foreign Affairs isn't up to it."

"That may be true, but it wasn't that simple," Michael said. "It's a very complex issue, with all sorts of fallout."

Michael rarely disagreed with her, largely because he lacked interest in the big issues. But this time he was proved right, as the rare negative public reaction from the GoodLord faithful demonstrated.

In the longer term, while the national loss of face was painful, Sylvia could see the advantages of an Australian foreign policy with reduced ambitions overseas. Sylvia was sharply aware that there were more immediate problems to solve, and where New Guinea was concerned, at least it was now off the list of Pacific neighbours who kept demanding assistance.

Freddie Wu agreed with her that there was a strong case for "cutting your losses". Australia was a large enough continent for a policy of self sufficiency to make sense.

The immediate issue, though, was to reduce the fallout from this disaster by somehow getting Zelda to shut up about it, as well as all her usual complaints. However, Sylvia concluded, it would be counterproductive to kill her, given the problems that arose after Sam Newbold's death.

In some ways it could be more satisfying to incapacitate Zelda, so that she would be out of action, perhaps in ill health, in a situation similar to Michael's first wife, Isobel. That was also a delicate situation, given that Isobel was Michael's first wife. The police would have grilled everyone in close proximity to her if she was murdered.

In Zelda's case, if she was put out of action with something that looked like an illness while she was overseas, then she would be totally harmless, and no suspicions would be aroused as they would by her sudden death.

***

When Sylvia spoke to Freddie about ways and means of removing Zelda from the political scene, he was sceptical.

"She's such a public figure," Freddie said. "She's grotesquely right wing in her opinions, of course, to the point where her ideology overcomes her self interest. However, she has grassroots support as an iconic Aussie larrikin, as you know."

"Yes, that's true," Sylvia said. She didn't often disagree with Freddie, although their discussions were always robust. "But at the same time, she is causing real damage to public perceptions of our Government."

"You are right," Freddie said, "but what can you do about it?"

"Do you have good contacts in Singapore?" she asked.

"Of course," said Freddie, just as she expected. "Why do you ask?"

"As you know, Zelda is going to the Global Rare Earth Minerals Conference in Singapore next month. And I'm thinking of organizing a little surprise for her there. Zelda needs to be removed from the scene."

"That would suit a large number of my colleagues in the mining industry," Freddie said. "Her monopoly of mineral exports is a real problem."

"Excellent. We need something that will encourage her to retire from the public scene, something that looks like an illness, but affects her enough to make her pull her head in."

"Leave it with me," Freddie said. "We have a month to work things out. There will be all sorts of opportunities at a huge international conference. So many people, so much activity."

***

One afternoon a month later, Freddie invited Sylvia to his apartment. Once Fong had served them coffee, he switched on his laptop and showed the screen to Sylvia.

As they sipped their coffee, social media lit up with reports of Zelda Freestone taken ill at a lunch hosted by the Brazilian contingent at the Global Rare Earths Conference in Singapore. Then a newsflash appeared on one of Marcus Gore's TV channels.

"Early reports indicate that Zelda Freestone, the Australian mining billionaire, was taken ill during the Rare Earths Conference in Singapore. According to eyewitnesses, Ms Freestone has been taken to hospital with symptoms indicating a stroke," a newsreader said.

Soon afterwards they watched videos of Zelda being carted on a trolley through the Emergency entrance to a hospital, her face shrouded in an oxygen mask.

"We must send flowers," Sylvia said, expressionless, and Freddie chuckled.

"Remind me never to become your enemy," he said, offering her a slice of cheesecake.

"What's the prognosis?" Sylvia asked.

"Reliable sources tell me that she will be mobile again within a few days, but that she will experience recurring episodes with symptoms similar to a stroke, possibly for the rest of her life."

"That's very unfortunate," Sylvia said.

"She will also experience regular bouts of exhaustion and shortness of breath."

"That's a well-informed source you have there."

"Of course," Freddie smiled.

"What's the impact on the share price of Freestone Corporation?"

"Going over a cliff as we speak."

"I see," Sylvia said. "I'm sorry to hear that."

***

Victor Rojo, after living by himself for a while after Eileen's death, became engrossed in a new life with his second wife, a spritely seventy-year old called Phyllis Patel. She had so much money in her own right that there was no way she could be accused of gold digging, something that Naomi had raised in her first conversation on the phone with Sylvia, decrying the fact that "Father was making a big mistake."

On the contrary, it seemed to Sylvia, Victor had finally found domestic happiness. Good things had come to him late in life, both his wealth and a wife who loved him with no reservations.

Phyllis Patel was an Anglo-Indian widow who had enjoyed a successful business career in Melbourne. She was a loud cheerful woman, not at all overawed by acquiring a stepdaughter who was the President's wife, nor for that matter a stepson-in-law who was President.

Victor moved into Phyllis' mansion in nearby Black Rock. Sylvia was relieved that Father was finally a happy man, basking in the attention that Phyllis lavished on him, cheerfully hosting regular dinner parties at home after decades of subjection to Eileen's moods, and her lack of any real friendships.

She visited Victor and Phyllis on a regular basis, always an enjoyable experience that made her ponder what it would have been like to have had a happy childhood family life.

Victor was well into his eighties now, and had blithely disobeyed his doctor's order to moderate his diet and take more exercise, so that his sudden death did not come as a shock. Nor was Sylvia concerned that Victor had left everything to Phyllis. It amused her that her brother Jack was livid that he now, in effect, worked for Phyllis as CEO of Victor's supermarkets. It didn't seem to occur to Jack that he was lucky to have any job at all. And Naomi, despite living in the lap of luxury with her dull but rich husband, somehow thought she was in dire need of a cash injection from Victor's estate.

The final straw for Jack and Naomi was that Phyllis was in charge of the funeral.

"What did you expect, for God's sake?" Sylvia said to Naomi on the phone. "She was his wife for several years."

"It's not right," Naomi fumed. Sylvia just laughed. It was ridiculous.

Mercifully Phyllis managed to brush off all this kerfuffle, inviting her step-children to join her and her two sons at Victor's funeral, a formal service in her favourite church, stage-managed so that there was no opportunity for disgruntled step-children to make a scene.

Only an official GovMedia film crew was there to record proceedings, something that Phyllis appreciated in order to avoid overwhelming crowds coming to goggle at the burial of the President's father-in-law.

"It will be nice to celebrate Victor's life in our own way," Phyllis declared, proving her point with a raucous party disguised as a wake, with a crowd of mutual friends happy to follow Phyllis' injunction to see Victor off in style.

The champagne flowed, a jazz band played upbeat standards, fond stories of Victor were told, and Naomi and Jack were forced to put up with it all, while Sylvia and Michael joined in the festivities, which ended with a resounding chorus or two of "For

He's a Jolly Good Fellow," sung to Victor's framed photo standing in its place of honour on the band's piano.

"Unconventional, and bloody good fun," Michael declared afterwards. "The right sort of send off. I'd like that for me when I cark it, if that's OK with you," he said to Sylvia.

"My pleasure," Sylvia laughed, knowing that Michael had no idea that she planned to step into his shoes as President the moment he drew his last breath, if not before.

CHAPTER 14

HARRY

In the dimly lit vacuum of fear and despair we all inhabit now, President Fontaine has become the shining light on the hill, showing the nation the way forward to a bright new future.

GoodLord's growth shows that Fontaine's move to the presidency is the best recruitment tool any Pentecostal preacher could ever have devised.

"All will be well!" he declares on prime time TV. "Join GoodLord and help to rebuild our wonderful country!"

The vast majority of people seem to feel reassured by his positive messages. President Fontaine now has little competition, as all political opposition disappears from the national stage.

GoodLord Inc, my new employer, is the fastest growing corporation in Australia, at a time when businesses are tanking on a daily basis. We have offices pretty much everywhere now, well staffed by professionally qualified people, plus call centres and a powerful online presence that makes GoodLord accessible in every home across our vast continent, as big as the USA, from Perth to Brisbane, and Hobart to Darwin.

A great many of the new recruits are responding to Michael Fontaine's call to join GoodLord out of patriotism as much as religious belief, in the effort to build a new Australia, necessary, as he insists in his TV appearances, to a secure and prosperous future for the country and its people.

It's clear to me not only that Michael Fontaine believes every word of this pious nonsense, but also that no one around him thinks that it is any more than a brilliant public relations gambit.

***

The Ministry for National Security and Home Affairs under Noah Kowalski is also growing fast, making its presence felt with widely publicized raids on criminal gangs and terrorists by heavily armed guards hired from security firms.

The regular security meetings that Noah asks me to attend give me access to what is happening at the highest level of GoodLord Inc, and coincidentally, give me plenty of info for Neil Bautervich. I can now move beyond feeding Neil tidbits about Noah's gambling and GoodLord office gossip, to something more juicy.

The meetings are chaired by Sylvia Fontaine in her role as CEO of GoodLord, with Anna Kalajian in tow, plus Michael Fontaine when he's available. I'm surprised to see Charlotte Hung in attendance too. Now that she's emerged from the wings and into the limelight I can see how much I underestimated her. For the most part she doesn't say too much, but when she does she certainly makes her point.

Mainly, though, I'm fascinated by Sylvia Fontaine's exercise of power, and Noah's efforts to assert himself as Fontaine's right-hand man, rather than just third in line after Sylvia Fontaine.

"The increasing flood of refugees into the cities is a threat to law and order on a huge scale," Noah says in one of the meetings held at GoodLord HQ. "We need to contain these vast crowds of people," he adds. "They are destitute and they have no ID."

"Are you suggesting internment camps?" Sylvia Fontaine asks, raising an eyebrow.

"Not at all," Noah says. "We can't staff internment camps at present anyhow. However, we can expand our system of Protection Barriers. At the moment the Barriers are simply checkpoints placed in strategic locations. But in Melbourne, for example, if we used the M80 ring road as our line in the sand, we could erect barbed wire fences to stop refugees entering the city. Then build facilities in the regions to cope with their needs."

"So rather than interning them, we lock them out?" Anna Kalajian says.

"Exactly," says Noah. "And provide for them outside, as I said. More effective, better for the people involved. It will also improve security inside the Protection Zones, to call them that. It will give us more security against looting and terrorism. We can't allow the random attacks on our security forces to grow into organized disruption."

Everyone around the table nods approvingly. Noah is certainly making a big impression on his new party.

"But how will we fund a project of that size, Noah?" Michael Fontaine says. "The cost will be enormous."

"Certainly," Noah says, "however, the bonus is that it will be a massive construction project nation-wide, providing jobs for thousands of workers."

It sounds like a version of apartheid to me, but it's obvious that they are going to go for it. There's so much room for unintended consequences with this sort of stuff, it's hard to know where to begin, but none of them care about that.

"We'll need to improve our ID programs," Charlotte Hung says helpfully. "Then we could have total control over entry to Protection Zones. We could use DeepFaceID on smartphones to keep out everyone who is unregistered."

"Good idea, Charlotte," Noah says. "Something like DeepFaceID would simplify matters all round."

"Most of the people on the other side of the Protection Barriers wouldn't have smartphones, or DeepFaceID," I say. "Or mobile phone reception, for that matter. They've lost everything."

"Sometimes we have to make difficult decisions," Charlotte says in a mild tone of voice, as Noah chuckles and Sylvia maintains her poker face.

Charlotte has certainly got that right, except that the poor buggers on the other side of the barbed wire will suffer for it.

***

My first face-to-face meeting with Neil Bautervich after joining GoodLord is in a seedy motel room in a semi-industrial northern suburb near Tullamarine Airport, planes roaring overhead every few minutes or so.

The neighbourhood is littered with abandoned shopfronts, rubbish strewn everywhere, vacant allotments, no trees, all the usual signs of a downhill slide to urban oblivion now on steroids with the impact of the fires on this side of town. Roads are blocked due to damaged power lines, and some freeway overpasses severely damaged by intense heat.

"Things must be getting tough," I say to Neil, who is perched uncomfortably on a sagging bed, while I struggle with an ancient beanbag slumped against a battered wardrobe. The faded brown curtains match the worn carpet, and the sad little room smells like damp towels. "Can't your budget cover Poynton's Pub any more?"

"We have to keep on the move these days," he says. "We're confronted with sophisticated surveillance equipment and an army of people hired to follow us around."

"I thought that was your role."

"The change of Government is having an impact," Neil says. "We don't know who we can rely on any more."

That's unusually frank, coming from Neil. I've never heard him say anything negative about any Federal Government over the years, Coalition or Labour. After all, the security people are the puppeteers, not the puppets, or at least that's the general idea.

"Noah Kowalski's Ministry for National Security and Home Affairs is taking a new approach," Neil adds.

"You mean, doing its own thing?" I ask.

"Yes. Anything you can tell us about that?" Neil asks.

"He's going to ramp up the Protection Barriers, installing barbed wire barriers around the city, and demanding DeepFaceID for entry."

"When did this happen?"

"Approved in a meeting a couple of days ago," I say. "Going ahead very soon."

"God that's grim," he says.

"Yep. Apartheid all over again."

He doesn't really respond, just sits there staring at the wall. I have an eerie feeling that Neil is losing control of the situation, or his masters are. Then he says, "Is Fontaine behind this?"

"Hell, no. My impression is that Michael Fontaine is genuine," I say. "That is, what you see is what you get. He's a preacher, he believes in his hokey religion, he likes people, he likes to be liked. A simple soul, really. The ideal ringmaster for a circus like GoodLord."

"But he's not in control?" Neil says.

"The people in control include Sylvia Fontaine, with Freddie Wu lurking in the shadows. And now Noah Kowalski. He's like a rat up a drainpipe in his new job. It's as though Noah has found his calling, and it's bringing out his inner Hitler. The three of them, Sylvia, Freddie and Noah are driving this juggernaut. They're hoovering up rabid fans, who are as loyal to GoodLord as communists or fascists were back in the day. They don't need a nasty little bastard like Hitler. They've got their favourite uncle up there on stage, Michael Fontaine, telling them that Jesus loves them, that they deserve to be happy, and all will be well. And they are completely free in this new democratic republic, so long as they do what they are told."

"Christ!" says Neil. "It's a coup! Just like when the CIA got rid of the Whitlam Government in 1975."

"You mean, you believe the CIA actually knocked off the Australian Prime Minister back then? They engineered the Dismissal?"

"Whatever. For God's sake, Harry, I know that you think national security is a farrago of lies, but this is important. Find out what these fucking bastards are up to. Sylvia Fontaine. Freddie Wu."

I think that this is the first time I've heard Neil swear. It makes me laugh as he glowers at me, then he pulls a bottle of brandy out of his briefcase, finds two glasses in the bathroom, and pours us both a drink.

"It's obvious what's going on," I say. "Michael Fontaine does whatever he's told to do. Limiting the freedom of the press in the name of not upsetting folks with more bad news, for example. However, it's difficult to find out the details of how it all works. Most of it happens behind closed doors, with Sylvia Fontaine pulling the strings with Freddie Wu."

"They're getting too powerful, too fast," says Neil. "The new Ministry for National Security and Home Affairs is taking advantage of the damage done to our personnel and computer systems by the fires to start their own security service. Answerable to no one except GoodLord. That will give them total control."

"At this stage of the game it's going to be tough to stop them," I say. "GoodLord has real momentum now."

Neil nods glumly and pours us both another shot of brandy, and settles back against the head of the bed.

"OK, you focus on whatever you can bring me from the meetings you attend."

"Fair enough. But next time we meet, I would prefer that bar you took me to last time in Collins Street," I say. "We need more upmarket meeting places like that. Why not let me line up our next venue? Maybe we could join a nice golf club and pretend to be golfing buddies. Spend a bit of time at the nineteenth hole."

Somehow Neil manages a tight smile. It's difficult to see the funny side when you know without a doubt where the country is headed.

***

The bad news keeps on coming. Billie passes away one night in hospital, after a brief bout of pneumonia. Rita and I have been visiting her regularly, and there she was, chirpy and bright every time without fail, pleased to see us.

She died quietly in her sleep, apparently, the perfect death, if you can say that. The only good thing to me is that she lived to a decent old age, outliving Sid by many years, the poor bugger dying soon after retiring from his factory job.

The strange part of arranging Billie's funeral is the complete lack of her relatives to contact, just like Sid when he died. When I try to chase up Billie's sister to give her the sad news, I can find no trace of her or her family in Adelaide at all, not even on the internet. Maybe they left town, or even went overseas, who knows.

CHAPTER 15

SYLVIA

Michael Fontaine moved his breakfast tray and reached for the remote as the newsreader on TV commented on footage of crowds of refugees in the Wastelands trudging along a dusty road carrying their belongings. Men, women and children, exhausted and frightened, they had been turned away at a Protection Barrier for lack of the required ID.

"Thousands of people are struggling to find food and water," the newsreader was saying, as Michael switched off the TV.

"This Protection Barrier business is going to lose us support before too long," he said gloomily. "I don't know if we should have let Noah have his way with that idea."

Sylvia cocked her head and looked at Michael attentively.

"I think you'll find in the long run that Protection Barriers will be very popular, darling," she said. "They make people feel safe."

"For the people on this side of the Barriers, maybe," he replied. "There's going to be a hell of a lot of people on the other side up in arms before too long…" Michael trailed off, reaching for his coffee with a doleful look on his face.

"Deten Inc is doing a marvellous job building all the Barriers. And you have to give credit to their security company, too. They're managing the riots extremely well," Sylvia said to Michael. "That news report was too graphic. It should never have gone to air. We need GovMedia to get on top of things, make sure the news gives our point of view."

"You mean censorship?"

"Yes. It's all manageable, given the right approach," Sylvia said.

The solution was obvious. Hand over all news media issues to GovMedia. Then appoint Marcus Gore, the largest news media baron in Australia, as CEO. That gave him a complete monopoly as the entire news media came under GovMedia's control, with a brief to shut down all negative press. Very soon, with Marcus Gore in charge of GovMedia, the situation improved immensely.

Meanwhile, inside the Barriers, the general population seemed to approve of the measures taken to protect them, with no publicly expressed opposition to Government policies.

***

Sylvia still enjoyed her intermittent catch-ups with Freddie Wu, one of the constant pleasures in her life. They would sit up in bed discussing matters of state, particularly the strategies for maintaining control of a fluid and unpredictable situation in the chaos of climate change, mass homelessness, and growing terrorism.

"We're under immense pressure," Sylvia said. "The huge building projects to repair freeways, housing, hospitals and schools are well behind schedule. The level of destruction is overwhelming."

"Yes," Freddie said. "It's a moment of truth, right enough. Faced by countries all around the world. On the other hand, you have a powerful grip on Government and enough minerals to keep the economy in good shape for another hundred years."

"I hope you're right. I'm worried about unrest outside the Protection Barriers. Riots and terrorist attacks are increasing."

"You're already benefitting from Deten Inc's assistance in building the Protection Barriers," Freddie said. "Perhaps you could call on them to assist in establishing detention facilities for terrorists and applicants for the Protected Zone? They have a proven track record in managing detention centres for asylum seekers and criminals."

"Yes, that sounds like a very good idea," Sylvia said. "Do you have contacts in Deten Inc?"

"Of course, the CEO is a good friend of mine. Let me introduce you to her. Fatima Salah. Brilliant woman."

"Thank you," Sylvia said. What came to mind immediately was the need for a new Ministry for Incarceration to manage the new detention centres, free of Noah Kowalski's influence.

The final step was to suggest to Michael that the ideal person for the position of Minister was, of course, her trusted colleague, Anna Kalajian.

***

"I think we should reopen Pentridge prison," Sylvia said to Anna Kalajian. "Remember what an image Pentridge had back in the day? Those thick bluestone walls, the guard towers? Site of the last public hanging in Melbourne? And right in town, a symbol of how seriously this Government takes law and order. And that would mean strong oversight from the Ministry for Incarceration."

"It's mostly a museum now, isn't it?"

"Yes, totally wasted. This is a high priority, a special project. Somewhere to imprison high profile detainees and dissidents, for example. Think of how names like Guantanamo Bay or the Lubyanka strike fear into the hearts of dissenters and terrorists."

"I see what you mean," Anna said. "A visible threat and very secure."

"Also, we'll need special facilities for interrogation rooms and so on. I have some information from Freddie Wu for the latest in detention technology. Ankle bracelet alarm systems for every prisoner. State of the art surveillance systems. We'll use Pentridge as a holding station before prisoners are sent to Phillip Island."

"How do you want me to approach this special project?" Anna asked.

"Form two project teams, one for Pentridge and one for Phillip Island. Keep Noah Kowalski informed, but not involved. As Minister for Incarceration, you will manage the whole project, with assistance from Charlotte on the finance aspects. Report directly to me."

"Thank you, I appreciate your confidence in me. When do I start?"

"Tomorrow. No time to waste. Work starts immediately. Top priority."

When Sylvia and Anna met Fatima Salah, the Deten Inc CEO, she was more than amenable to Sylvia's insistence on a reconversion of Pentridge and an immediate start to the Phillip Island detention facilities. Sylvia accepted Fatima's proposal to include security services in the contract, so that prison guards and other staff were part of the deal.

"Anna will be managing the project," Sylvia said. "I'll be leaving it in her capable hands."

"I think you'll find that it's an excellent package deal," Fatima said. "Our detention people have the very latest training, and they are well equipped."

As the project progressed, Sylvia was pleased to see that Anna Kalajian was flourishing with her new responsibilities as Minister for Incarceration, especially with such a high profile project to enhance her position in Cabinet. Anna was undeterred by verbal attacks from Noah Kowalkski, responding to all opposition diplomatically and calmly.

It only took a month of frantic activity to restore Pentridge to working order, at least as a starting point. Everything was still in place, all that was needed was some refurbishment to return it to its former Bastille-like old self.

Anna Kalajian made regular visits to Phillip Island by helicopter, reporting back on how the rough scrub was being transformed into the headquarters of Deten Inc's growing national system of detention facilities. The pace of construction was impressive.

"We'll be laying the foundation stone and opening the main headquarters building in a few weeks," Anna said in her regular report to Sylvia. "Who do you want to do the honours?"

"I'll be there, but I think that Michael and you should manage that. I'll stay in the background," Sylvia said. "You can introduce Michael's speech at the ceremony, in your role as Minister for Incarceration."

"Thanks," Anna said. "I appreciate it."

"An excellent job. Well done," Sylvia said.

**

The trip by helicopter to Phillip Island for the opening ceremony encountered turbulence the minute they took off. By the time they were flying over the Bay, Noah was sweating and looking bilious.

Sylvia had insisted that Noah attended the opening of Deten Inc's headquarters on Phillip Island, to rub in the fact that he had lost the battle over the creation of the Ministry for Incarceration to manage detention centres nation-wide. Of course Noah Kowalski, although knowing he was well and truly beaten, kept up a guerrilla war of contention and complaint.

Sitting next to Anna Kalajian in the helicopter, and facing Sylvia and Michael, it was obvious that Noah was feeling unwell. Sylvia knew that he was susceptible to air-sickness, and at the back of her mind it had occurred to her that a flight on a helicopter to Phillip Island might just give Noah something to think about. And after all, he could hardly refuse to perform his public duties with the excuse of travel sickness, given how much their role depended on constant visits to all parts of the country.

Sure enough, while they were still ten minutes away from landing, Noah hastily grabbed at an air sickness bag and vomited profusely into it, gasping and retching. After several heaves he sat back sweating and miserable, holding the full airsick bag to his chest like a nervous society matron hanging on tightly to her handbag in a disreputable part of town.

"You might need another bag, Noah," Sylvia said over the racket made by the helicopter, ignoring Anna grinning alongside him.

"Where do I put this one?" Noah gasped. Sylvia pointed under his seat, and he awkwardly bent forward and put the bag on the floor between his legs, then suddenly grasped for a new bag just in time to vomit again.

Michael leaned forward in his seat, concerned, and shouted, "You all right, Noah?" as Noah shook his head and groaned.

After they landed in a clatter of blades and a swirling cloud of dust, Noah tagged along in the rear of their party, wiping his sweating face with a handkerchief as they greeted Fatima Salah and her entourage of Deten Inc executives.

Fatima looked comfortable in the searing heat and dust of this rocky outcrop off the Victorian coastline, her regal composure more an outcome of a life of privilege and an MBA at Harvard than her Middle Eastern heritage.

"Nice to see you again," Fatima said to Sylvia and Anna. After Michael was introduced, Noah limply smiled a greeting, still gripping his handkerchief and rubbing his forehead.

"Noah is a little indisposed after our helicopter flight," Sylvia said.

"A glass of water for Mr Kowalski," Fatima instructed an aide. "Perhaps you would like to rest for a few minutes?" she added to Noah, and he was led away nodding gratefully to an airconditioned Range Rover.

They made a short trip in a convoy of SUVs to Deten Inc's imposing glass-coated corporate headquarters, set amongst palm trees partly obscuring a huge forbidding concrete building ringed with a high barbed wire fence.

"The new detention facility," Fatima said with a smile to Michael and Sylvia, waving a hand at the juggernaut the Fontaine Government had just paid many millions for.

"Yes, Anna has kept us informed with very detailed reports," Sylvia said with a smile.

"The very latest in detention technology," Fatima added. "The design enables total isolation and surveillance at every step a prisoner has to take within the detention centre."

"You have eyes on the prisoners at all times?" Michael asked.

"Not one prisoner is off our surveillance screens at any moment of the day," Fatima said firmly.

"Very impressive," Michael said.

"No terrorist can escape from here," said Fatima, and half a dozen aides nodded simultaneously, bursting with pride at this vision of the perfect model for incarceration.

The opening ceremony was elaborate, with lavish praise from both sides for the deal that had been made. Michael Fontaine in his introductory comments extolled the efficiency and reliability of Deten Inc. But it was Anna Kalajian's speech as Minister for Incarceration that trumped everyone else. The time was over, Anna said, for pointless acrimony between the private and Government sectors over what should be done to rebuild the nation. The Fontaine Government, she said, with this crucial deal with Deten Inc, was introducing a new policy of strategic alliances between Government departments and the private sector. These would not be ad hoc arrangements, but rather part of an overarching plan. The focus was on the common good, pooling the best aspects of both sectors, for the benefit of the nation as a whole.

These comments drew loud applause, not least from Sylvia, who had approved Anna's speech. Sylvia believed that with this new policy she had found a means of outmanoeuvring not only Noah Kowalski, but any of the wealthy and entitled moguls from the big end of town who felt they should be asked for permission by anyone who dared to trespass on their turf. Mercifully Zelda Freeman's strident advocacy of her opinions in opposition to the Government was now a thing of the past, as she lived the constrained life of a permanent invalid since her "health episode" in Singapore.

The new policy of strategic alliances was a happy arrangement all round. The corporate insiders had a legitimate means of tapping immediately into Government funds whenever a massive project was undertaken, while the Government had a strategy for managing Government handouts to wealthy and influential allies behind closed doors.

Fatima Salah responded with grateful thanks to a new Government that understood the need for total commitment to the safety of law-abiding citizens. Vision and stability were essential to economic growth, she stated, with a smile at Anna Kalajian, and it seemed to Sylvia that they had a new ally in the scheme of things. Anna would be the best choice to deal with Fatima Salah, clearly someone with a bright future, and as CEO of Deten Inc, a vital ally for the survival and success of the Fontaine Government.

Noah Kowalski didn't reappear until they were all seated at lunch in a vast dining room the size of an amphitheatre. He was still accompanied by an aide, who made sure he was supplied with a glass of water as he sat down at the table.

Noah glanced around with a sickly smile. "Back on deck," he said, and everyone expressed their sympathy.

"Will you be OK for the trip back to Melbourne?" Sylvia asked, and Noah frowned.

"I might rest up for the afternoon, and then get a lift back to town," he said.

"Good idea," Michael said. "Take it easy."

The lunch was excellent, and Sylvia could see that Deten Inc knew which side their bread was buttered on. The hospitality was first rate, and due acknowledgement was given by the hosts to the guests who had bestowed a billion dollar contract upon them, as a down payment, it was hoped, on many years of efficient management of the incarceration of terrorists and dissidents, and all threats to the peace of the Democratic Republic of Australia.

***

"I think that the new detention facilities we're setting up with Deten Inc will improve security outside the Protection Zone enormously," Sylvia told Freddie. "But I'm still concerned about security here, inside the Protection Zone. My own security included. We know that since Sam Newbold's death I've been under surveillance, and that is intolerable."

"It certainly is," Freddie said. "When our own security agencies spy on members of the Government, it raises the whole question of who is running the country."

"Yes. We still have too many security agencies from the old guard snooping around," Sylvia said. "Noah has made good progress in building up his Ministry of National Security and Home Affairs and reining them in, but they are still not under our control."

"Perhaps you need another new security agency, one that reports to you alone, with the goal of targeting the established agencies, and rooting out the old guard. You would clean out the top people, no point chasing after the small fry."

"An excellent idea," Sylvia said. "That will take a lot of resources and planning."

"As always, I am willing to help. A fascinating project." Freddie smiled, and called Fong for more coffee.

Sylvia was always struck by Freddie's ingenuity. He seemed to have a solution to any problem that came up, which would help explain his longevity in the brutal world of Chinese politics. Together with his total ruthlessness, of course.

CHAPTER 16

HARRY

"Unfortunately in my role as Vice President Public Relations for GoodLord I've come across some leaks to the press from inside our organization," says Anna Kalajian at one of our regular GoodLord security meetings.

"What leaks?" Noah says.

"I have a file of detailed examples," Anna says calmly. "The bulk of them can be attributed to information given to an editor in The Argus, called Neil Bautervich."

At the mention of Neil's name my ears prick up, and I struggle to stay expressionless.

"Who the hell is he?" Noah snaps.

"Please, Noah," says Sylvia, "let Anna explain what's happening."

Sylvia chairs these meetings with a light hand, but there is never any doubt who is in charge.

"Of course," Noah says between his teeth.

"Well," Anna goes on, "after extensive checking, I discovered that, unfortunately, the source is Harry Mott."

And Anna looks at me with a frown across the huge meeting table, while I try to fend off a panic attack. I'm so surprised I don't have to fake it.

"What?" I say, very loudly. "Is this a joke?"

"No, Harry, I'm afraid not," Anna says in her best school prefect's voice. "We can link certain leaks to the press to the timing of your meetings with this Neil Bautervich over the last several weeks, at Poynton's Pub in Carlton. I would like to submit the documentation."

"Certainly," Sylvia says.

It's obvious that this accusation is no surprise to Sylvia, although Michael Fontaine's mouth is wide open with shock. Charlotte Hung's expression is impossible to read.

"Good God!" is all Michael says.

Anna starts handing out stapled sheets of documents, and I flick through my copy which shows photos of me with Neil Bautervich having a few beers and a yarn. And that is what I say.

"That's me and an old mate from my university days having a few beers."

But then I go further into the documents, which have highlighted paragraphs from articles on GoodLord in The Argus, which Anna attributes to me. Close enough to be true, not something I had even considered as Neil and I gossiped about all sorts of stuff, some of it with security ramifications, most of it not. However, there is nothing in these highlighted articles that suggests anything like spying. Just tidbits of information about GoodLord that are enough to titillate public interest without crossing any lines involving security.

"Pretty trivial stuff, Anna, don't you think?" I say blithely.

"What the hell were you thinking, Harry?" Noah says. Then he turns to Sylvia, glancing at Anna, and adds, "I'm sure we can move on from this. It might be stupid, but it's not a serious security issue."

"I'm not sure about that," says Sylvia. "Maybe this is just scratching the surface."

That's typical of Sylvia, a great nose for betrayal, and her comment gives me a nasty sense of what might follow if they dig deeper. Charlotte Hung is still silent, but nods her head in agreement.

Anna also agrees with Sylvia, of course, and so does Michael Fontaine after lots of huffing and puffing, and "What were you thinking, son?" addressed to me across the table.

Noah, however, is boiling mad.

"This is just rubbish," he mutters angrily, flicking through the document. "I talk to journos all the time. They can be very useful, and you need them on side."

"It doesn't look like that is what is going on here," Sylvia says, looking straight at Noah.

It occurs to me after the shock has settled a little, that first, this is a near miss, and second, I should resign before they find out the real truth, that I'm a fully paid up informant to a Government agent.

Discussion continues about how trivial this is or not, and Noah gradually loses the battle, his voice louder as he is outmanoeuvred.

Sylvia continues to be suspicious, and Charlotte points out that I work for Noah, therefore the issue of my trustworthiness is Noah's responsibility. She seems to be suggesting that Noah should resign. So finally I toss in the towel.

"Look," I say, "I apologize. It was careless of me. But I understand that I've lost your trust."

I look at Sylvia as I say this, then at Michael Fontaine and Noah. I ignore Anna Kalajian and Charlotte Hung, both of them just a chorus for Sylvia's opinions.

"As it happens," I go on, "I've been thinking about retirement for a while now, for personal reasons. Wear and tear, the impact of work on my family. And so I'm offering to retire, quietly and no fuss, effective immediately."

"I think that's appropriate," Sylvia says firmly. "What do you think, Michael?" she says.

Her husband agrees, saying it is a pity to see me go, but he hopes I understand.

"Goddammit!" Noah roars, tossing the incriminating documents across the room. Best I leave as soon as possible, to minimize the fallout. I feel like I'm only a step away from the full truth coming out, with very real damage to Noah.

I say yes I do understand, apologize again, with a particular apology to Noah, as my boss, and leave the room.

As soon as I reach my office, a couple of security guards follow me in.

"I'm sorry, sir, you can't take anything with you," one of them says. He reaches for my laptop, but I stop him.

"Hang on a minute. I work here as an independent consultant. I don't even log on to the GoodLord system." This is true, but it makes no impression on the security guard.

"No problem, sir. We'll check out your laptop and return it to you in a day or two."

I am out of the building in ten minutes, empty handed, and set off in my car just on lunchtime.

***

What next? I take the scenic route home to Carlton, like a homing pigeon, flapping back to the comfort of the familiar scenes I have inhabited all my life. Down Beach Road on a sunny day, boats cheerily afloat at Brighton Marina, past Luna Park on St Kilda Esplanade, then through South Melbourne to the mess of freeway ramps that take me up the M1 and then the off-ramp over Bolte Bridge. I have enjoyed this drive in my time at GoodLord, but now I'm checking my rear view mirror to see if I'm being followed.

At the crest of Bolte Bridge, a view of Port Phillip Bay in the rear view mirror, window open to the breeze, Tim Buckley singing on the sound system. Nothing like a golden oldie. Hang in a wide circle back across Flemington and Parkville, and park alongside Princes Park in Royal Parade with a view of my alma mater, Melbourne University, or at least, the residential colleges that still dominate the northern end of the campus.

This has been my world since I was an adolescent, a skinny pimply kid shouting Maoist slogans and skipping lectures, feverishly reading every book I could get hold of as new topics grabbed my attention, getting hopelessly drunk in the endless pubs around the campus, skipping from one share house and brief relationship to another, before settling into grubby old Carlton, renting a little bedroom with a mattress on the floor. Now, of course, I own a fashionable house on this expensive inner city turf, inhabited by creatives and progressives with a spare million bucks or two.

After making sure that the coast is clear, I ring Neil Bautovich on the burner phone in the glove box.

"Neil," I say, "got some news for you. Can we meet for lunch? Café Lorenzo?"

"Sure. When?"

"Half an hour?"

"In a hurry, huh?"

"Yes."

"OK. See you there."

A little later I manage to grab a metered parking space near Café Lorenzo, and find Neil already inside.

I join him at a table down the back, and look at him for a moment or two wondering what to say.

"So what's going on?" Neil asks, tousled but stylish in a new suit, silk tie neatly in place. The aircon is working well since the recent renovation, and we have a nice view of Lygon Street with its neatly curated kerbside trees, café tables and tourist shops.

"I've been sprung at GoodLord," I say, "but in a strange way."

"How's that?" Neil says. He seems calm about it, businesslike.

After we order lunch, I tell him about Anna Kalajian's exposé of our meetings in Poynton's, and how she got it wrong, but it was enough to get me sacked. "That's why I suggested that we meet here," I say. "They could still have me under surveillance. Easier to spot them here than in Poynton's."

"Ah," says Neil. "So it all went to plan."

"What plan, for fuck's sake?" I ask, feeling irritated.

"Anna is one of ours," Neil says. "I shouldn't be telling you this, but it doesn't matter any more. She told me that routine surveillance by GoodLord was being carried out on you, and that they had some photos of us chatting in Poynton's. There was no way she could hide the photos from Sylvia Fontaine. I was expecting your call."

I sit silently fuming.

"We got Anna to cook up the story about your meetings with a journo to get you off the hook," Neil added. "Sylvia Fontaine was suspicious of you, and looking for ways to get one up on Noah Kowalski. The best result for us was to keep Sylvia Fontaine happy, get you out of GoodLord in one piece, and preserve my cover."

"Christ!" I say. "Why didn't you tell me?"

"That would have been too nerve-wracking for you, and would have required you to act the part when you were 'sprung', as you say. This way, you didn't have to act surprised."

"Thanks a lot."

"I knew I could rely on your natural talent for deception."

"Right," I say. "Preserving your cover being the main point of it all."

"It was dangerous for both of us. Think back to what happened to Sam Newbold when he got in Michael Fontaine's way."

"You mean Sylvia Fontaine and Freddie Wu's way. Michael Fontaine wouldn't have anyone killed."

"OK then. Those two. Basically they are running GoodLord, so, no difference there."

"Are you sure Anna's one of yours? She seemed very keen on nailing me for leaking to the press."

"I'm sure. Don't worry about it," Neil says.

We sit drinking our wine in silence until our meals arrive. As we eat, Neil starts talking again.

"We've had a good run, Harry, and we've got a lot of info on GoodLord. A job well done."

I think Neil is congratulating me, or trying to console me, I'm not sure which. Maybe both. Himself too.

"Yeah, and I'm out of a job."

"But look at what a fruitful career you've had," Neil says with a grin. "Imagine if you'd thrown a larger rock at Mona Lippi all those years ago, and killed the future Governor General outright! That might have meant no hope of a President Fontaine or a new republic. And you would've ended up behind bars. On the other hand, perhaps the experience of being hospitalized due to a violent demonstration drew Dame Mona into a life of public service, on the side of law and order! Which led to her appointing Michael Fontaine as interim Prime Minister. And unfortunately, we mustn't forget, leading to Dame Mona's suicide after she was sacked. Just look at the part you played in facilitating the rise of Michael Fontaine and bringing our beloved country the blessing of a republic! Talk about the butterfly effect! You know, a butterfly flaps its wings in Patagonia and causes a hurricane in Florida."

"Oh, crap," I say, "knock it off."

"On top of that," Neil continues, "you helped to bring Sam Newbold's lifelong career as a spy for China to an end by delivering that package to him and giving his killer the opportunity to bump him off. And not forgetting that you played a vital part in encouraging Chinese influence through political donations, hurrying on the demise of our corrupt mainstream political parties, and saving China the bother of plotting an outright coup, like the CIA's coup against Gough Whitlam in 1975. All that China had to do was finance Michael Fontaine's rise to power. No coup necessary."

I look at him gobsmacked, and begin to ask, "Are you saying..." but Neil just smiles benignly at me.

"I propose a toast," he continues, "I really do, to Harry Mott, the unseen and unloved benefactor of the brand new Democratic Republic of Australia!"

Neil then raises his glass in a mock toast, smiling widely, while I give him a two-finger salute across the table. In all our years of fandango in various meetings, this is Neil at his most sarcastic. I might have proposed a counter-toast to his own shadowy contributions to modern Australian history, but I let him enjoy the moment. It's the beginning of the end for both of us after all, and Neil goes on to confirm exactly that.

"It's time to retire," he says, putting down his glass. "The security services are being taken over by Noah Kowalski's Ministry for National Security and Home Affairs anyway. Our systems and networks are being systematically destroyed. I'll be pulling out Anna Kalajian as soon as it's safe to do so. Which is going to be tricky. She might even have to change identity. Then I'll be leaving."

"What will you do?" I ask. "Take up fly fishing? Recreational hang gliding? Go overseas?"

I have no idea what Neil's life is like. Whether he lives a patrician lifestyle in a Toorak mansion with prestigious dinners to attend, or a simple backstreet life in suburbia. Is he married, or in whatever relationship? Is he gay? Does he have kids? Or even a dog? Total mystery.

Anyway, he doesn't reply, just saying, "You'd better retire too. Or get some job in a totally different area. Working for charity, perhaps. Retirement is best, though. They lose interest in you once they see you going to the 7-Eleven in your slippers in the morning for a loaf of bread and a packet of cigarettes."

"I've given up smoking."

"I know," Neil says. "But I'm guessing you'll take it up again when you've retired."

"Very amusing," I say.

On the one hand you can argue that Neil's entrapment of me when I was a student ruined my life. On the other, it's true that he rescued me from a boring desk job and set me on a more interesting and lucrative course. Thrills and spills, with more cash, even if it does leave me looking over my shoulder for the rest of my life.

Anyway, that is that. We finish our meal, have a coffee, shake hands and say goodbye.

Later in the day Noah Kowalski rings me, and we have an awkward conversation. He's still fuming about Sylvia Fontaine's unrelenting war on him.

"She's trying to isolate me every way she can," Noah rumbles. It's all about him, of course, and my sudden ejection into a forced retirement doesn't feature at all in his rant about the injustice of it all.

I let it all go over my head, waiting for him to finish, and finally he says he's sorry to see me go, and I say thanks and goodbye. I've been his trained monkey for more than twenty years, and I've got no doubt that he'll replace me before the end of the week and I'll never hear from him again. In a month's time he'll be struggling to remember my name. Such is life in the bear pit.

In the meantime, I'm hoping that Sylvia Fontaine will be satisfied with her most recent victory over Noah Kowalski, and leave me to my own devices now that I've been kicked to the kerb. No doubt she will soon be embarking on a new attack on Noah, and hopefully she'll see me as just some roadkill along the way to the total power she's craving for.

Nevertheless, I can't help thinking that Sylvia Fontaine won't be giving up any time soon. I'm beginning to understand Melissa

Frankel's story about how Special Branch surveillance made Sam Newbold so nervous while he was hiding out as a draft resister against the Vietnam War. Even the thought of constant surveillance is hard to deal with.

CHAPTER 17

SYLVIA

The list of Sylvia's personal enemies was getting longer by the day. GoodLord Inc had grown into a large and complex organization with powerful factions, and the people of influence within the Government were becoming too obstreperous. It was time to reassert control.

Out there somewhere were the remnants of the old security forces who had placed her under surveillance, fishing around in the aftermath of Sam Newbold's murder. No doubt hoping for a return to the old politics and the comfortable establishment that they had nested in like vultures for so long.

"We need a presidential security force reporting to us personally, something that we can totally control, Michael," Sylvia said after dinner one evening at Raheen. "There are too many people who are beginning to go their own way."

They were having coffee in the study at Raheen, a large room lined with bookshelves but dominated by a giant TV screen, with Michael glued to a football match between Richmond, the team he barracked for, and Collingwood, their old arch enemy.

A lot of Government money had been ploughed into keeping the Australian Rules football competition alive, a popular move across the country, designed to "keep up the community spirit".

"A presidential security service?" he said, glancing at her briefly. "Surely that would duplicate Noah's Ministry of National Security?"

"We need something like the old Secret Service in the USA, totally loyal to the President, before their Government collapsed," Sylvia said. "Security forces all around the world are notorious for going their own way. Even against their Government. This could easily happen with our Ministry for National Security and Home Affairs. At the very least, we need agents that report to us, people we trust, on matters we need to keep confidential."

"Sounds complicated," Michael said.

"We can keep it simple," Sylvia said. "We can place the service in the President's Office, and I can run it out of that."

"Let's think about it," Michael said.

Lately Michael had been digging his heels in more often, as he grew into his role as President. She allowed him a moment of assertion, letting the matter drop for the time being.

She sought Freddie Wu's advice on how to set up the new presidential security service, and received a detailed blueprint from him. The service would liaise with the Ministry for National Security and Home Affairs when necessary, but report only to the President. At least on paper. In reality it would report to Sylvia.

"When it comes to surveillance and security checks, my advice is to start with your own people," Freddie said to Sylvia. "There are bound to be internal breaches of security amongst your staff, and you need to weed them out before you start anywhere else."

It sounded like good advice, and Sylvia intended to apply it to the full.

***

It didn't take long for Sylvia to find the right candidate to head up the new security service in the President's Office.

"A good choice," Michael said, acquiescing to Sylvia's selection of a bright young Army officer called Vijay Gatz, with a background in Military Intelligence and service in the New Guinea border conflicts. He appeared to have the nous and initiative she was looking for, as well as athletic good looks and a way with words.

"Well, Major Gatz. How would you like to head up this new security service I'm thinking of?" she asked him in the informal interview she arranged, just the two of them. "Protecting the President and myself. But with a larger remit across broader security issues."

"Excellent," Vijay Gatz replied. "Just what I was hoping to find after my discharge from the Army."

She liked the look of him, and gave him the job with total responsibility for setting up an independent security service that would answer only to her.

Vijay Gatz set up the new service in record time, before Noah Kowalski could do anything to block it. He recruited veterans from the military services and former police officers, as well as technical and professional support staff. A rigorous training program was initiated, using Freddie Wu's blueprint to mould an elite force of dedicated agents.

It was a satisfying outcome, and all the insiders in GoodLord understood the power that Sylvia now wielded; her own security services enabled her to do as she saw fit. Noah Kowalski could complain all he liked, it was too late.

***

Once Vijay Gatz was comfortably settled into his new role in charge of security in the President's Office, Sylvia briefed him on the immediate priorities she had for him.

"One thing I must explain, Vijay. Our first task is to screen our own," Sylvia. "Regardless of their status or length of service."

"I understand," Vijay said. "It's the best way to go."

She was pleased with his ready grasp of the issues, and the speed with which he was adapting to his new role.

"His experience in military intelligence is ideal for the job," Sylvia told Michael.

"I'm surprised that Noah didn't snap him up," Michael said.

"I think Vijay likes the idea of a direct link to the President," Sylvia said.

"Good for him. I need bodyguards I can trust."

Bodyguards weren't Sylvia's first concern, but she conceded the point. Amidst the ongoing chaos, anything was possible from an aggrieved population outside the Protection Barriers, all of them with nothing to lose. Nonetheless, it was essential to begin close to home.

"I have a list of names of the people you should start checking," she said to Vijay. "In particular, Noah Kowalski, Minister for National Security and Home Affairs. After all, the head of national security must be verified beyond all doubt. And Noah's close associates. One of them, called Harry Mott, used to work for him as some sort of consultant. Mott was reported by Anna Kalajian for associating with a journalist here in Melbourne, and was sacked for giving him inside information. The journalist is on the list too. His name is Neil Bautervich, and I suspect he worked for the old security agencies."

"Yes, Ma'am," said Vijay, taking the list she handed over. "Should I detain Bautervich, or initiate surveillance first?"

"Surveillance, I think," Sylvia said, smiling at Vijay's willingness to go for broke.

"Certainly, Ma'am," Vijay said.

***

Vijay's initial surveillance report on Neil Bautervich was a model of insight and efficiency.

"So as you can see, Ma'am, our surveillance showed no recent contact between Neil Bautervich and Harry Mott. Bautervich's registered address is a fake. In fact he lives with a woman called Melissa Frankel. They seem to be like an old married couple, they spend a lot of time together."

"Thank you, Vijay," Sylvia said. "Excellent work." She liked Vijay's casual ruthlessness. His appearance reminded her of her mother's favourite movie star, Cary Grant, in the old Hitchcock movies on TV.

"What would you like me to do next with this case?" Vijay asked.

"What do we know about Bautervich?"

"He had a successful career in journalism, on one of the old Marcus Gore newspapers. Recently retired. Everything about him indicates long-term involvement in security activities, probably in a senior position."

"What could we get out of him?"

"Well, he could know to what extent GoodLord has been penetrated by the old security services. And he could also have useful information more broadly about the identities of his handlers and other agents."

"And what about this woman he lives with, Melissa Frankel?"

"Evidently she has a long track record as a human rights lawyer. She's semi-retired now."

"Excellent. I think we should ask Mr Bautervich some questions. And Melissa Frankel."

"An arrest then?"

"Yes, both of them. Take them to Pentridge, to begin with. See how Bautervich responds, use the Frankel woman to apply pressure on him. Then depending on early results, I think with an arrest this promising we will want to transfer him to Phillip Island for more intensive interrogation."

"Yes, Ma'am."

"And Vijay, I would like to come along on this occasion. I would like to see the arrest take place."

"I'll make the necessary arrangements, Ma'am. However, I must say it might involve a lot of waiting around in the heat."

"I've lived a varied life, Vijay. That won't be a problem."

"Yes, Ma'am. I didn't think so."

***

After an hour sitting in the back of Vijay's SUV just after dawn while he spoke sporadically into his mouthpiece, Sylvia was already wondering if this escapade was the best use of her time. She suppressed the urge to ask what was happening, and gazed out the window at the affluent suburban street, filled with Edwardian villas under a canopy of kerbside trees.

After a murmured conversation on Vijay's radio, he told her that things were on the move. Three agents moved silently along the pavement in front of the target house, and apparently three more had been sent to climb over the back fence.

"He's in there with his girlfriend," Vijay said. "I doubt he'll offer any resistance. Bautervich is getting on a bit these days. He won't get far if he makes a run for it."

Sure enough, after a brief conversation at the front door of the house, the agents walked Bautervich and Frankel over to the SUV, both wearing maroon silk pyjamas and dressing gowns, with bare feet, and in handcuffs.

Vijay wound down the window, and greeted them.

"Good morning. We'd like a word with you both, if you don't mind coming with us."

"I do mind," Bautervich said, "but of course that makes no difference."

"No, it doesn't," Vijay said.

Bautervich was a thin, elegant man with a defiant look, unshaven, grey hair tousled from sleep. Frankel was grey haired, in her sixties at a guess, an attractive woman still, her expression angry and contemptuous.

"We need to get some clothes," Frankel said.

"Don't worry about that," Vijay said. "You'll both be inside Pentridge and wearing prison overalls within the hour."

"Who's that in the back with you?" Bautervich said. "That's a familiar face."

"None of your concern. More to the point, why are you giving out a false address, and hiding here in your partner's house?"

Bautervich scowled at Vijay, and Sylvia could see that, as was often the case with men hiding secrets, a woman would be his downfall.

"Take them away," Vijay said, and the agents marched Bautervich and Frankel over to their van and bundled them into the back.

"This should be very interesting," Sylvia said. "Maybe Frankel is a spy too. Let me know when they are ready to talk. I want to hear what Bautervich has to say about Harry Mott. I'm sure that there's some unfinished business we need to sort out."

ABOUT THE AUTHOR

James Garton lives in the hills outside Melbourne, Australia. His novels include *Maltese Twist*, *Holus Bolus* and *Farrago*.

www.ingramcontent.com/pod-product-compliance
Lightning Source LLC
LaVergne TN
LVHW040050080526
838202LV00045B/3560